Snowflakes, Cupcakes & Kittens

Novels in the Guiding Emily Series

Guiding Emily

The Unexpected Path

Over Every Hurdle

Down the Aisle

Novels in the "Who's There?!" Collection

Deadly Parcel

Final Circuit

SNOWFLAKES, CUPCAKES & KITTENS

BOOK 3 IN THE PAWS & PASTRIES SERIES

BARBARA HINSKE

CASA DEL NORTHERN PUBLISHING

ISBN: 9798987694213

Library of Congress Control Number: 2023909318

Casa del Northern Publishing

Phoenix, Arizona

To Linden Gross—our remarkable collaboration has made my writer's journey a joy.

CHAPTER 1

$\mathcal{C}$lara flung out her arm to stop the screeching alarm on her cell phone. She'd woken hours ago at one a.m. and her racing mind hadn't let her fall back to sleep. She was glad it was finally time to get up.

Noelle shifted onto her side and sighed heavily, burrowing her muzzle into the down-filled duvet.

Clara rolled to face the terrier/dachshund mix whom she had adopted (or was it the other way around?) and planted a kiss on the top of her head. "I know you'd love to sleep in, but bakers have to start their day at three a.m. Especially on a big day like this one. With any luck, Valentine's Day should be insanely busy for us."

She threw the covers back and padded to the bathroom, the cold tile floor on her bare feet vanquishing any remaining sleepiness. Clara turned on the water to the shower and the tiny room was soon enveloped in a thick cloud of steam.

Her thoughts raced in happy anticipation as she contemplated the promise of the day ahead. The patisserie she'd dreamed of owning since she was a girl would be ready to open by the end of the month. The beautiful Sweets & Treats sign—with the shop's name in a flourishing font sitting atop a fluted cake stand next to a bouquet of forget-me-nots—took her breath away every time she saw it jutting out over her display window. A "Coming Soon" banner in the window made her pulse quicken.

Clara had been operating her bakery since the beginning of the year from a building she'd leased from Johanson's Diner. She'd purchased all the equipment she would need from Josef and Maisie Johanson when she'd taken over the diner's bakery business. That equipment would be moved to her new location the following week. Her bakery display cases and the high-end coffee machine were already installed.

She adjusted the water temperature and stepped into the steamy shower. The hot water relaxed her muscles, stiff from the exertion of the eighteen-hour days she'd been putting in as she prepared to launch her business.

Every member of Maisie's talented baking staff had stayed on to work for her. They'd happily integrated Clara's new ideas and offerings into the items they'd been baking for the diner for many years. The dedicated "From Sweets & Treats" display case that Josef and Maisie had installed in the diner, offering a rotating array of items for sale, had been a resounding success and had garnered Clara a devoted following.

During the past week, that case had offered red velvet strawberry cupcakes, heart-shaped sugar cookies iced in an intricate filigree pattern, chocolate-covered strawberries and cherries, and Linzer hearts with raspberry jam, dusted with powdered sugar. They'd sold out of everything in the case during the breakfast rush on the first day. Even though they had increased production every day since, they were still sold out by late afternoon.

Her staff had come to her four days earlier with a genius idea. She would supply a modest amount to the case in the diner on Valentine's Day and the diner would direct customers to the new Sweets & Treats location once they'd sold out. Maisie and Josef endorsed the idea with great enthusiasm. It would be the perfect way to introduce customers to her new location. The staff had happily agreed to work double shifts the next three days to produce enough baked goods.

Clara rinsed the last of the shampoo from her hair and shut off the water. She snaked her hand through the slit in her shower curtain and grabbed her towel, rubbing her skin vigorously before wrapping her hair in the towel. She still couldn't believe her good fortune in meeting these kind and generous people who now felt like family. After mourning the death of her beloved mother and surviving the recent divorce from her cheating husband, she finally felt like the dark cloud that had clung to her had dispersed and she was living in sunshine.

Clara shrugged into her robe and padded into the kitchen to press the start button on her coffee maker. She whistled to Noelle and waited by the back door for her dog to abandon her cozy spot on the bed and make her way to the door. "Come on, girl. While we're young," she said, as her usually lively companion made her way slowly to the door.

Noelle planted her bottom at Clara's feet and looked up at her with baleful eyes.

Clara opened the back door just enough to allow Noelle to access the steps into the fenced yard. "I know it's cold, sweetheart," Clara said. "You'll have to go out there without me. I'm only wearing my robe and my hair is wet." Clara sighed in exasperation. "Go on, girl," she said firmly.

Noelle got slowly to her feet and did as she was told. Instead of tearing around the yard, sniffing out the perfect spot to do her business, she squatted at the bottom of the steps, then returned quickly to where Clara waited behind the door.

"It's not that cold out there, is it?" Clara asked, noticing Noelle's lack of enthusiasm. "Let's get you fed. I need to finish getting ready and head out." She scooped kibble into Noelle's bowl and set it in the customary spot on the floor. "I'm going to work a very long day today, so Ian will come over to let you out before and after school. He'll take you for a walk this afternoon. I'll be home before my date tonight. Kurt's making dinner for us at his place."

Noelle stood over her bowl and picked at a piece of kibble.

Clara poured herself a mug of coffee and switched off the machine. "I have an actual date on Valentine's Day. It's been years…" Her voice trailed off as she headed to her bedroom with her steaming mug.

Clara launched into her morning routine of drying her hair and applying a minimal amount of makeup while she sipped her coffee. Her baker's uniform of black slacks, white shirt, and sturdy lace-up shoes required no decision-making. She never wore jewelry when she was working, so she didn't stop at her jewelry box. She made her bed with four swift, sure motions.

Clara hurried through the kitchen, placing her empty mug in the sink.

Noelle still stood at her bowl, gingerly eating her kibble.

Clara stopped short. "That's not like you." She went to her furry companion and knelt beside her. "Are you okay, sweetie?" She stroked the top of Noelle's head.

Noelle took the last bite of kibble and crunched it, wagging her tail.

"That's a good girl. Ian will be here by seven. I'll see you later." She gave her beloved dog one last pat before standing and heading for the front door. Clara grabbed her coat, purse, and keys from the coat rack in the tiny foyer and headed into the frigid darkness.

CHAPTER 2

Clara pulled her car into the parking lot between Johanson's Diner and the one-story block building behind it that had served as the bakery for the diner for decades. At four a.m., the lights were on and two other cars were in the lot. She shook her head; she shouldn't be surprised that Joan—her head baker—was already here. Joan was as excited about today's soft launch of Sweets & Treats as she was.

The other car belonged to Josef. He regularly arrived at the diner that bore his name at five for their six a.m. opening. This was extra early for him. His wife Maisie had operated the bakery until health issues had convinced them to sell it to Clara. Now Maisie was a silent partner in the patisserie. Josef and Maisie were both committed to the patisserie's success.

Clara hurried to the door and was met with a fragrant cloud of steam as she stepped inside. She recognized the almond notes in the aroma. Joan was making more of the heart-shaped Linzer cookies that she, Clara, and Maisie all thought were their best offering.

Maisie sat on a high stool behind one of the long worktables. She held a piping bag and was bent over a cooling rack of sugar cookies, applying an intricate web of decoration on the pink and red iced cookies.

Clara hurried to the older woman who she loved like a mother. "Maisie! What in the world are you doing here—at this hour?"

Maisie kept her eyes focused on the task at hand. "I couldn't sleep. Neither of us could, actually. Both Josef and I were tossing and turning. He finally asked if I minded if he came in a little early this morning." She chuckled. "I said I didn't mind one little bit—as long as I could come with him." She finished piping icing onto the last cookie on the rack and leaned back to admire her handiwork.

"These look amazing," Clara said.

Maisie nodded in satisfaction. "They're not as good as the ones you do. You're better with a piping bag than I am."

"That's not true."

Maisie raised her eyes to Clara's. "It is true, but I'm still pleased with these."

Joan rolled a rack of Linzer cookies out of the commercial oven, then joined Maisie and Clara.

"I thought we weren't going to make any new products for Sweets & Treats today," Clara said. "We finished up everything yesterday."

"That was the plan when I went home yesterday afternoon," Joan said. "I went to bed extra early and woke up at one. I tried to go back to sleep, but it wasn't going to happen. I was too eager to get in here. I figured I'd make up another batch of the Linzers. We'll sell out of them for sure. Maisie got here shortly after I did, and we decided to make more sugar cookies."

Clara looked at the two older women opposite her. If her car hadn't broken down on the highway, forcing her to stop in Pinewood, she would never have found this place. Or these incredible people who shared her vision and were working so hard to make it a success. Her vision grew cloudy, and she blinked away sudden tears. "You are both going home by mid-morning." Her voice was firm.

Joan opened her mouth to protest.

"I appreciate you both—more than I can say. I'm not going to work you to death! The rest of the bakery crew will arrive in under an hour. The only things they should bake today are the standing orders for the diner. We've got enough Valentine's Day items for the Sweets & Treats case at the diner and for the patisserie itself. If we sell out, that won't be a bad thing."

"I couldn't agree more," came a familiar male voice from behind her.

"Josef. I didn't hear you come in," Clara said.

The stocky older man with the shock of white hair approached them with steaming cups of coffee in each hand. "I brought these for Joan and Maisie," he said. "I'll go back and get you a cup."

"Thank you, but I've already had the one and only cup I'm allowing myself."

"You should come over to the diner for breakfast and to see the Sweets & Treats case. It looks fabulous," he said.

"I think I will. It'll probably be the only meal I eat all day—at least until dinner," Clara said.

"Is Kurt taking you out?" Maisie asked. "It is Valentine's Day."

"I wasn't sure when I'd finish my day," Clara said, "so he's making dinner for us."

Maisie's eyebrows shot up. She spun to face Josef. He shrugged. "That's so nice, dear," Maisie said.

"I'm bringing red velvet strawberry cupcakes for dessert. This is exciting. I've never had a man fix a meal for me before."

"Your ex didn't cook?"

Clara shook her head. "He was happy to leave all of that to me. How about the two of you?"

"We're going to that cozy Italian place on the square—right around the corner from the patisserie. We've celebrated Valentine's Day there for years," Josef said.

"I'm glad you're treating yourselves to a meal out," Clara said.

"I'll go scramble some eggs. You'll need protein for the day ahead. Then you can load the baked goods into the delivery van and head over to Sweets & Treats," Josef said.

"That's a great idea," Clara said. "Joan and I can handle the patisserie on our own, so we can drop Maisie at your house on the way."

"It's a plan," Joan said, putting a protective arm around her friend's shoulder.

"And let the two of you have all the fun of opening up Sweets & Treats for the first time? Not on your life! I'm an owner, you know." Pride tinged her words.

"All right, but you're to remain seated and let Joan and me ring up orders and make coffee." Clara locked eyes with Maisie. "You'll be an observer, which will actually be very helpful. Joan and I will be too busy to notice anything that isn't working well."

"Exactly," Joan interjected. "We'll be running around—at least I hope we'll be busy enough to be running around—and won't be able to focus on what we can do better."

"And I'll pick you up after the breakfast rush and take you home," Josef said. He turned toward the door. "Follow me. I'll have you fed and out the door in twenty minutes."

"We'll open the patisserie at seven," Clara said. "That'll give us plenty of time to unload the baked goods and place them in the cases."

"Do you think we'll need more help than the two of us?" Joan asked.

"I wouldn't think so. We didn't do any advance advertising. All we'll have is a sandwich board sign on the street that says 'Now Open.' We'll be relying on foot traffic. It should be fine. I just hope we sell half of what we've made!"

CHAPTER 3

*M*aisie grinned at Clara. "We're ready. It's time."

Clara made one last tour around Sweets & Treats, inspecting the bakery cases, straightening the displays, and removing a smudge on the chalkboard menu with her thumb.

"It all looks beautiful," Maisie said. "Everything's perfect."

"You've done it!" Joan gushed.

"We've done it," Clara corrected. She picked up the sandwich board sign. "Time to unlock the door and set this on the street."

"Wait," Joan said, pulling her cell phone from the back pocket of her slacks. "Let's get a picture of the two of you." She motioned to the long display case along the wall under the menu. "That'd be a good place for you to stand."

Clara set the signboard against the wall and joined Maisie at the display case.

"Here we are, ladies, on the opening day of what I'm

sure will become another legendary Pinewood business," Joan said.

Maisie and Clara slipped their arms around each other's waists and smiled at the camera as Joan snapped photos.

Joan scrolled through the photos she'd taken. "We've got some great ones here. I'll forward them to you both later."

Maisie pulled Clara into a tight hug. "I thank God, every day, that you came into my life," she whispered into her younger partner's ear.

"I do the same," Clara whispered back. "I'm so glad we're in this together."

"I think we may have our first customer," Joan called from the front of the patisserie.

Maisie and Clara released each other.

Clara picked up the signboard, unlocked the door, and stepped onto the sidewalk.

Kurt Holbrook waited for her there, with an enormous bouquet of red and pink tulips in a cut crystal vase.

"Kurt," Clara cried in delight. She quickly positioned the signboard at the edge of the sidewalk and returned to him, kissing him squarely on the mouth. "I didn't think I'd see you until dinner tonight."

"I wouldn't miss the chance to wish you good luck on the day you opened Sweets & Treats," he said. "These flowers are for your opening, too." He held out the vase.

"You're the most thoughtful man in the entire world," Clara said. "I've never seen more beautiful Valentine's flowers."

"I remember you said tulips are your favorite. And

they're not for Valentine's Day. That comes later. This is for your opening."

Clara took his arm and ushered him inside. "Have I mentioned that you're perfect? Let me get you a cup of coffee and anything you'd like from the cases."

"I'll take the coffee, but I'd like to order a box of some of everything to bring to my office. That'll make me the favorite attorney there."

"If I had to guess, I'd say you already are." Clara smiled at him as she picked up a large pink bakery box and began filling it with an assortment of the cookies. She placed a dozen red velvet strawberry cupcakes in their own box and finished up with a box of chocolate-covered cherries and strawberries. "This should assure that everyone has a sugar rush before mid-morning." Clara stacked the boxes and pushed them toward him.

He handed her his credit card, and she shook her head. "On the house."

"That's nonsense. You can't stay in business that way." He turned to Maisie and handed her his card.

"I learned long ago not to argue with this one about money," Maisie said, running the card through the reader. She handed the card and receipt back to Kurt. "Thank you for being Sweets & Treats' first official purchase."

"Exactly how I wanted to start my day," he said.

The door opened behind him and the owner of the guitar shop next door stepped inside. "I'm so glad you're open," said the lean older man. "I plan to get my coffee here every morning—on one condition." He raised his brows and looked at Clara with mock seriousness.

"We're happy to help in any way," Clara said, cocking her head to one side.

"You don't let me buy cookies or pastries more than a couple times a week. I've worked hard to keep the weight off—doctor's orders—and I don't think I should start a croissant-a-day habit now."

"We'll hold you to it," Maisie said. "You can count on us. We're going to be the kind of place where we know our regulars' orders before they even walk through the door."

"That sounds wonderful," the man said. "Welcome to the neighborhood." He ordered his coffee as he perused the display cases. "Since this is your first day, I think I will order something else."

The door opened again, and two women stepped inside.

Joan helped their neighbor with his selection.

"You're hopping, and the place hasn't even been open for five minutes." Kurt leaned close to Clara and kissed her cheek. "I've got to run. See you tonight. Text me when you're on your way over and I'll fire up the grill. We're having steak. And—thank you for the coffee."

One of the women waved to Clara from the other end of the display case.

"Go," Kurt said. "You're going to have a great day."

Clara smiled at him and stepped up to greet her customer.

CHAPTER 4

*K*urt tore his eyes from his computer screen. The pinging of his cell phone told him he had a text message. It wasn't even two o'clock—he didn't expect to hear from Clara until later in the afternoon. Still—he couldn't help but hope.

Today a roaring success! We sold out of everything here and at the diner. My staff even made extras. I'll be done on time, so let me know when you want me to come over. Xoxo

The motion he'd been half-heartedly working on would have to wait. Right now, he wanted nothing more than to implement his plan for a romantic Valentine's Day dinner with Clara.

Flowers and a balloon bouquet were in place right inside his front door. A sapphire-blue cashmere scarf was waiting on his dining table, nestled in silver tissue paper tucked into a silver gift bag tied with red satin ribbon.

All that remained was to prepare a home-cooked meal. He bit his lower lip and sucked in air through his teeth. He'd never made a meal in his life.

Clara had been so excited when he'd invited her to dinner at his house. He'd never said *he* would be cooking. She'd just assumed and gone on and on about how inept her ex was in the kitchen. Kurt's common sense had gone out the window. In that moment, all he'd wanted to do was show Clara how different he was from Travis. He'd acted like a high school boy trying to impress a girl. Kurt raked his fingers through his hair. Now he'd have to produce a home-cooked meal. Still—how hard could that be?

He tapped out his reply.

Outstanding! Something else to celebrate. See you at 5?

Her response was immediate.

Sure! C u then!

Kurt opened his search engine and typed in "Valentines' Day dinner recipes." The internet promptly presented him with seventy-nine million results. He clicked links. Kurt grabbed a legal pad and began a list of ingredients. He squinted at a recipe as he read the instructions. What in the world was parboiling? Maybe cooking was harder than he thought, but he knew where to go for help.

Kurt slapped the lid of his laptop shut, tidied the papers on his desk, and headed to the front door. "I'll be gone the rest of the day," he told the receptionist as he strode by.

"Thank you, again, for the goodies from Sweets & Treats," the woman said. "Everyone's been talking about how good they are."

"Glad you enjoyed them. Spread the word around town, will you?"

"Of course. The owner is… your friend?"

"Both the owners are my friends. Thank you. Have a good evening."

"You, too."

Despite the frigid temperature, Kurt felt warm as he hurried to his car. It had been years since he'd celebrated the holiday with the woman he loved. He and Rachel Johanson had been deliriously happy together—right until she'd died after a lengthy battle with cancer.

He'd gone to a dark place after that—cutting himself off from others and telling himself he'd never marry again. Thankfully, his kind in-laws had not allowed him to fester in despair. Maisie and Josef had included him in their lives —almost against his will in the early days after Rachel's death. Their shared grief over Rachel's death had forged an unbreakable bond. That they had encouraged him in his relationship with Clara—in fact, practically insisted upon it—meant the world to him.

He got into his car and placed his call. Maisie would tell him how to produce his foolishly promised home-cooked dinner.

Kurt pulled grocery sacks from his back seat and raced up the steps to Maisie's kitchen door.

She heard his footsteps and opened the door before he had the chance to knock.

He leaned in and kissed her cheek. "It's so nice of you to bail me out like this."

"I love both of you like my own," Maisie said. "I'm happy to do it. But what in the world was going through your mind—letting her think you can cook?"

"Momentary insanity," Kurt said. "I was so eager to

impress her that I lost my mind." He removed a huge bouquet of roses and calla lilies from the top of one of the sacks and handed them to Maisie.

"Let's get these into water so they don't wilt before you can give them to Clara," she said.

"They're for you," Kurt said.

"They're lovely, but you'll want them for Clara."

"I've already taken care of that. These are for you—to thank you for helping me. And to bribe you to keep my secret."

Maisie grinned. "Not necessary. I won't give you up." She filled a pitcher with water and inserted the flowers. "You spoil me. Thank you. I'll arrange these later. We need to get busy."

"I got everything you told me to. I want you to sit over there," he gestured to the kitchen table, "and instruct me. That way I won't feel like a fraud when I take credit for making dinner."

Maisie took her seat. "I had a couple of baked potatoes on hand, so I put them in the oven after you called. Take them out now so they'll be cool enough to handle."

"Right," Kurt said, picking up the potholder on the counter and removing the potatoes. "They smell great already."

"They'd be fine with sour cream, butter, and green onions, but making them into twice-baked potatoes elevates the meal."

"We all know that I'd only serve an 'elevated meal.' " Kurt looked over his shoulder at Maisie and grinned.

"While they cool, you can chop the ingredients for the salad."

Kurt pulled a knife with a long serrated blade from Maisie's knife block and picked up a head of romaine.

"Do you have knife skills?" Maisie asked.

"Sure. You pick up a sharp knife and start cutting."

Maisie got to her feet. "Let me show you." She took the knife he was holding and returned it to the block, selecting an eight-inch utility knife. "First, this is how you hold a knife in your hand." She gripped the heel of the blade with her thumb and forefinger, and wrapped the other three fingers around the handle. Maisie demonstrated the way to curl the fingers of the other hand away from the blade as she chopped.

Kurt watched with rapt attention. "You're really fast with that thing."

Maisie placed the knife on the counter and stepped back. "I've been doing this for decades. Now—you try it. And go slowly. You don't want to bleed all over your beautiful salad."

"No, ma'am," Kurt said. He set to the task, chopping and rinsing the ingredients until he'd assembled a colorful salad.

Within the next hour and a half, Kurt had prepped the salad and made a balsamic vinaigrette to dress it with. Twice-baked potatoes were ready to reheat in the oven and two thick filet mignons had been seasoned.

"So—I'm all set for the meal," Kurt leaned his back against the counter and rested his palms against the edge. "I just need to know what to do with the appetizer."

"That'll be easy. Cut the baguette you bought into half-inch slices. Spread some of the fig spread onto each one, then cover that with a smear of the softened cream cheese.

Slice some of those dried figs into thin pieces and add those to the cream cheese. Top with a pinch of microgreens and drizzle with balsamic vinegar. You've got yourself a yummy—and very foodie-looking—hors d'oeuvre."

"This will knock her socks off." Kurt bit his lip. "I feel like a fraud. If you hadn't helped me, I wouldn't have known how to do any of this."

Maisie rose and came to his side. "The point is, you did do it. There's nothing wrong with taking credit for it. No one is born knowing how to cook. We all have to learn."

"You're a great teacher, Maisie. Calm and patient." He put his arm around her shoulders and hugged her. "Thank you for letting me barge in on your afternoon."

Maisie sighed. "This is just what I needed this afternoon. They shooed me out of Sweets & Treats this morning. I came home, feeling very sorry for myself. I'm used to being busy. Instead, I'm at loose ends. This cheered me up more than you know."

Kurt pulled back and looked into her eyes. "You need to discover what your next chapter will be."

Maisie nodded. "I've recovered from my stroke. The doctor says I can return to my normal activities, but Josef is terrified I'll have another one. I suggested that I help at the diner, but he won't hear of it."

"I'm sorry that you're feeling this way—and that I didn't notice."

Maisie cuffed his arm. "This isn't something for you to worry about. I'll sort myself out. What you need to do is load this delicious meal into your car and go home to get ready for Clara."

"I guess you're right." He grinned at his accomplice. "I'll let you know how it goes."

"You'd better!" She planted a kiss on his cheek. "I have no doubt that tonight will be a complete success."

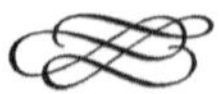

Ian Ramsey slung his backpack into the corner of the kitchen. "I'm home, Gran," he hollered as he crossed the large foyer into the front sitting room of the old Victorian mansion where he and his mother lived with his great-grandmother.

Tabitha Trent sat in her favorite over-stuffed chair by the bay window. She rested the book she was reading on her lap and took off her reading glasses. "How was school?"

"Fine."

"Did you exchange Valentine's cards in your class?"

"We don't do that anymore in sixth grade, Gran."

"Well… that's too bad. It's a nice tradition. To tell the people around you that you care for them."

"Yes, ma'am."

"You seem in a bit of a hurry."

"I'm anxious to go check on Noelle," he said. "She wasn't herself this morning. I guess I'm a little worried."

"You're very responsible about that dog," Tabitha said. "I'm proud of you. Go see to her."

"Do you want me to bring you your tea before I go to the guest house?"

Tabitha shook her head. "Take care of Noelle first. I can wait. I wouldn't want anything to happen to Clara's dog. They're the sweetest tenants we've ever had. We'll have tea together when you're done."

Ian turned quickly and raced out the back door, letting the screen bang behind him.

He was ten feet from the door of the guest house when he knew something was wrong. Noelle's muzzle wasn't peeking between the lace curtains filling the small bay window at the front of the house. He didn't hear her muffled, excited bark emanating from behind the door as he inserted his key.

He pushed the door open. "Noelle." He called again. "NOELLE." He ran to the kitchen at the back of the house, hoping he'd find her at her water bowl. She wasn't there.

A frisson of fear ran down his spine. He checked the back door. It was still firmly closed. She couldn't have gotten out.

He turned and began his search. She wasn't in the living room. "Noelle," he called in a gentle voice. He didn't want to scare her.

His search of Clara's bedroom turned up nothing. He went through the other two bedrooms, to no avail. He stood in the hallway that ran the length of the house, his palms pressed against his temples, wondering what to do now, when he heard it. The gentle whimper of an animal in pain.

He spun around and listened harder. The whimper came again.

He raced into Clara's room and got down on his hands and knees.

The whimpering grew louder.

Ian crawled in the direction of the sound and found Noelle wedged under the far corner of the bed by the nightstand. He reached out a hand to the pathetic creature.

"Hey girl. It's me. What's going on?"

Ian tried to worm his way under the bed. "I need you to come to me so I can help you. Okay, girl?"

Noelle opened her mouth and panted. Her breath was fetid.

Ian recoiled but didn't retreat.

"Something's wrong with your mouth, isn't it?"

Noelle whimpered.

"Do you want to come to me? As soon as Clara gets home, she'll take you to the vet. They'll fix this." He hoped they could fix whatever was causing this sweet creature so much pain.

"Come on, Noelle." He patted the carpet a foot in front of her. "You can do it. Come to me."

Noelle began an Army crawl forward.

Ian cooed and encouraged until the furry creature was out from under the bed.

Noelle stood and shook herself, then immediately sank onto her belly.

"I'm going to put you in a blanket and carry you up to my house," Ian said. "I need to call Clara and I won't leave you here, alone. Do you understand?"

Noelle thumped the carpet with her tail.

"That's a good girl. You're so smart." Ian pulled the blanket off of Clara's bed and wrapped it around the suffering animal. He hoped Clara wouldn't mind that he was using it. He didn't think she would.

He got to his feet and carefully scooped up Noelle, bringing her to his chest. "It won't be long now, girl. I'll hold you until Clara gets here."

Ian made his way slowly back to the house, taking great care not to jostle Noelle. Cradling the pup, he placed his call to Clara.

CHAPTER 6

His cell phone announced the incoming call was from Clara. Kurt grinned as he scooped up his phone and tapped the screen to answer the call. "Hello, gorgeous."

"Kurt," Clara said, "Noelle's sick—really sick!"

"What's wrong?"

"I'm not sure. Ian just called and I'm on my way home now. He was holding her and I could hear her whimpering."

"Can you get her into the vet?"

"No. I called them as soon as I hung up with Ian. They're booked for the rest of the day. They referred me to an emergency vet clinic on the far side of town."

Kurt turned off the oven that was preheating for the potatoes, shoved the steaks that were resting on the counter back into the refrigerator, and grabbed his jacket and keys before she'd finished her sentence. "I know exactly where it is. I'll pick you up at your place in ten minutes."

"You don't have to do that. I can manage…"

"You're not going alone. End of story. Drive safely and try not to worry. The doctors at the clinic are first rate. They'll take care of Noelle."

Clara swallowed hard. She certainly hoped so. The sound of Noelle's suffering had been heartbreaking; the thought of losing her was unthinkable.

She pulled into the driveway and parked next to the kitchen door.

Ian was at the kitchen window, watching for her.

Clara took the steps to the door two-at-a-time. "Noelle," she cried as she flung herself into the room and rushed toward Ian and his precious bundle.

Noelle stirred at the sound of Clara's voice and pointed her nose in Clara's direction. Her eyes telegraphed the depth of her misery.

Clara placed a hand on top of Noelle's head and gently rubbed between her ears.

Noelle panted and Clara gasped. She looked up at Ian. "Whoa. I see what you were talking about. Her breath is foul." She took a half-step to the right. "There's a swollen area beneath her left eye, too." Clara reached out a hand and gently wiped a drop of gooey discharge from beneath the swelling. "This is puss."

"How could she have injured her face?" Ian asked.

Clara shrugged. "I don't know. Sometimes stuff happens."

"Are you taking her to the vet?"

"Yes. Her doctor couldn't see her today so we're going to the emergency vet clinic. Kurt's driving us. He should be here any minute."

"Good. I hate that she's so miserable." Ian's voice was full of his own distress.

Clara put her hand on his arm and looked him in the eyes. "You've been wonderful to her, Ian. I'm sure that you cradling her until I got home has been extremely comforting."

He swallowed hard. "I hope so."

"Noelle knows how much you love her, Ian. I'm sure of it." Clara stepped back. "Do you mind holding her a few minutes longer? I should move my car—I'm blocking the garage. Your mom won't like that."

"I'm sure Mom won't care at all, under the circumstances, but I'm happy to keep holding her."

"I'll be right back. I brought you and your mom and Tabitha something from the patisserie, too. For Valentine's Day." Clara retraced her steps quickly, moved her car, and was heading back to the main house with a pink bakery box bearing the Sweets & Treats logo in hand when Kurt pulled into the driveway.

"I'M sorry this is taking so long," Clara said. "We've been here almost two hours."

"They're busy tonight, that's for sure. At least she's fallen asleep."

"Noelle was so nervous when we came in. I thought she was going to have a heart attack, she was trembling so hard."

Kurt shifted in his chair carefully under the weight of

the slumbering dog. He didn't want to say anything, but his left leg was falling asleep.

"Do you want me to take her?" Clara asked.

"Definitely not. We don't want to disturb her."

"I know you'd planned a lovely evening for us. I'm sorry we've ruined it for you."

Kurt cupped her chin with his hand. "The only thing I need to make this a perfect evening is to be with you. Everything else is beside the point."

"That's the most romantic thing anyone's ever said to me." She leaned toward him to kiss his cheek when Noelle's name was called by a veterinary technician at the entrance to the hallway leading to the exam rooms.

Clara shot to her feet and waved at the tech.

Kurt rose slowly, taking great care not to jostle Noelle.

"We're going to exam room number three," the tech said. She ushered them into the room and directed Kurt to place Noelle on the exam table.

Clara stood next to the table, keeping her comforting hands on her pet, while the tech took Noelle's vitals and entered pertinent information into a computer.

"What do you think?" Clara asked. "Will she be okay?"

The tech smiled. "The doctor will be in shortly. I'll let her go over everything with you. I've got a pretty good idea what this is—we'll have Noelle feeling fine in a few days." She quickly exited the room.

Clara swayed and braced herself against the table.

Kurt jumped to his feet and put his arms around her. "You've been up and on your feet for the past sixteen hours, haven't you?"

Clara nodded.

"Did you eat anything?"

"Breakfast. At four a.m."

"Exhaustion, hunger, and extreme emotional distress. Our next stop may be the emergency room—for you."

Clara leaned her head back against the solid comfort of his chest. "I'll be fine. I'm so glad you insisted on bringing us here." She closed her eyes. "I'm not sure I'd have been able to drive home safely."

He planted a kiss on the top of Clara's head and the three of them waited for the vet.

The young woman breezed into the room with an apology for their wait and an efficient manner. She made a quick examination of Noelle with gentle hands.

"I believe she has a broken left fourth upper premolar. It's severely infected and will have to be removed once a complete dental exam and X-rays confirm my suspicion."

"What about the pus-filled lump under her eye?" Clara asked.

"That's consistent with an abscess of the carnassial tooth."

"This all came on so suddenly. She was fine yesterday and even ate her breakfast today."

"Again, that's common. Your regular vet will be able to perform the needed exam and extraction. We'll send you home with an antibiotic and pain medications to make her comfortable until you can get her into her vet."

"She's so miserable. How long will they take to kick in?"

"We'll start her on her first dose here. She'll be more comfortable before you go to bed tonight. She may even act like she's back to normal tomorrow. Don't believe it. An abscess won't heal itself and can lead to more severe health issues. You need to have this tooth treated right away."

"Will she still be able to eat afterward?"

The vet chuckled. "You won't have to worry about that. Dogs are devoted to eating—it's part of their survival instinct."

Clara relaxed her shoulders. "You're telling me she's going to be fine?"

"I am. If you follow our instructions and give her the medications we'll send you home with, this will all soon be behind you."

"Thank you so much," Clara said, her voice cracking with emotion.

"The tech will be right in with your prescriptions. She'll show you how to give pills to a dog if you don't know."

She smiled at Clara, patted the top of Noelle's head, and hurried to her next patient.

Fifteen minutes later, Kurt gently placed Noelle onto Clara's lap in his car. A soft snore emanated from the blanket.

"Those pain meds must be kicking in," Clara said. "She's zonked."

Kurt helped Clara buckle her seat belt.

"They were so nice there, weren't they?" Clara asked. "I think I should take them cookies—maybe frosted sugar cookies. I think I have a cookie cutter that looks like a paw." She yawned, turning her head to one side since she didn't have a free hand to cover her mouth. "Gosh—sorry about that."

Kurt crossed to the driver's side and slid behind the wheel. "That sounds like a really nice thing to do. They'll love it. I've got a meeting on this side of town at the end of the week. I can drop them off for you, if you'd like." He pulled onto the street and waited for her response.

Clara didn't answer.

He glanced over at her. Clara's chin was tilted forward and her chest rose and fell with her rhythmic breathing. Both of his companions on Valentine's Day were sound asleep.

Kurt smiled to himself. If he had described to a friend how his evening had gone, they would have offered their sympathy. In truth, he felt like the luckiest man in the world. He'd found another caring, purposeful woman with whom to share the ups and downs of life.

CHAPTER 7

Clara rolled over in bed and cracked an eye open. A bright ribbon of light snaked up the center of her blackout curtains where the panels failed to overlap. She lunged to her feet. Her alarm was set for three a.m.—it was never light out at that time.

She swung wildly to the clock on her nightstand. She gasped, blinked, and looked again. 9:30. They'd left the emergency vet shortly after nine. She vaguely remembered Kurt helping her and Noelle get situated when they got home. That meant she'd been asleep for almost twelve hours.

Noelle. The thought hit her like a bucket of ice water. She wasn't in her usual spot on the bed, next to Clara. How was her sweet girl doing?

Clara made a fast stop in her bathroom, shoved her feet into her slippers, and went in search of her furry companion.

"Noelle?" she called as she rounded the corner into the hallway.

A quiet "woof" from the living room told her where to look. Clara stopped short in the entrance, surveying the tranquil scene in front of her.

Kurt sat on the camel-colored leather sofa, his feet propped up on the coffee table, and his hands poised over his laptop. Noelle was nestled against his right leg. Sun filtered through the sheer curtains at the bay window and illuminated a swath of the camel, coral, and teal patterns of the Aubusson rug. Kurt had lit the gas log and flames glowed in the warm stone fireplace.

"Hey, sunshine." He brought his feet to the floor and set his laptop on the coffee table. "You're up."

Noelle thumped her tail against the sofa, but made no attempt to move.

Clara raked her fingers through her long mane of chestnut hair. "What're you… what's going on? I should have been at work hours ago!" Her voice contained a note of panic as she crossed to the sofa and sank down next to Noelle.

The dog wagged her tail with enthusiasm.

"She seems much better," Clara said, leaning over to plant a kiss on Noelle's head. "Did you give Noelle her morning dose of medicine?"

"I did. She takes pills like a champ. And she ate her breakfast just fine. I found her kibble in the cupboard."

"Thank you for that. I'm so relieved she's getting better." Clara got to her feet. "I need to get out of here."

Kurt reached out and drew her back down. "You're taking the day off. It's all arranged."

"Oh?"

Kurt nodded.

"I've clearly been out of the loop. You'd better explain."

"Let me get us both a cup of coffee and I'll fill you in."

Clara relaxed into the back of the sofa, and Noelle crawled into her lap.

"Be right back," Kurt said.

Clara had no intention of taking the entire day off, but she had to admit—it felt wonderful to have slept in. She looked down at herself. She'd slept in her clothes from the day before. The last time she'd done that was when she'd stayed with her mother in the hospital on the day she died. Clara shook her head to dispel the sad memory. Her mother had left her enough money to open the patisserie and a note encouraging her to use the money to do something she would love. Tears pricked the backs of her eyes. She hoped her mother could see the happy life she'd created.

Kurt entered the room with two steaming mugs of coffee.

Clara smiled at him as he handed her a mug. "Thank you. Now—the last thing I remember is tumbling into bed. I think you told me you'd take care of Noelle?"

"That's right. You were asleep before your head hit the pillow. Both of you also slept the whole way home from the vet."

"I'm a terrible Valentine's Day date, aren't I?"

"Don't be ridiculous. Yesterday wasn't your fault, and—for the record—I had a great time. Anyway, Noelle needed another dose of medicine at midnight, so I stayed here to tend to her."

Clara noticed he was in the same clothes he had been wearing the prior evening. "Did you sleep here?"

He nodded. "This sofa is very comfortable. I think it's a better napping sofa than mine, and I didn't think that would be possible."

"I'm not much of a napper."

"You're missing out on one of the true joys of life. But back to yesterday: I called Maisie right after you went to bed. She said she'd contact Joan and the two of them would handle the bakery today. Since you're starting to move the equipment to Sweets & Treats tomorrow, you'd planned to scale back operations today. Maisie insists you're to take the day off."

Clara shook her head. "I can't dump all this on them. I have to go to work."

"Maisie said you should rest up while you can. You'll have to take over tomorrow, but they can easily handle today."

Clara and Kurt locked eyes over the rims of their mugs.

"Maisie issued strict orders that I'm to keep you away from the bakery today. You should already know this about me—I do everything Maisie asks me to do." He flashed his boyish smile.

Clara's gaze softened. "That's incredibly nice of her." She drew a deep breath. "I know the world won't come to an end if I take a day off."

Noelle looked between them and thumped her tail.

Clara raised an arm over her head and stretched. "It feels good to start the day slowly."

"So you're in agreement? I don't have to worry about you slipping out the back door while I've got my head turned?"

Clara chuckled. "No. I won't try to give you the slip."

"Excellent."

"Don't you have to work today?" Clara asked.

"I didn't have any court appearances, so I was able to clear my calendar. I thought we'd both play hooky today."

Clara grinned. "I love the sound of that. So—Ferris Bueller—what do you want to do?"

"There's a beautiful creek not too far outside of town, near my grandfather's old farm. I used to play in it as a kid. I still go out there at least once a season. Time seems to stand still there."

"Sounds lovely."

"I thought we could pick up sandwiches and drive out there for a picnic. It's a beautiful day. The sun's warm. Shouldn't take more than two or three hours. After that we'll come back here, pick up Noelle, and have our Valentine's Day dinner at my house."

"That sounds perfect. I'll call the vet to get Noelle's dental procedure scheduled, then shower and change clothes."

Kurt stood and pulled her to her feet. "I'll go home to pull myself together."

She slipped her arm around his waist and they walked to her door.

She tilted her head back and he kissed her. "I'll be back here inside of thirty minutes."

"I'll be waiting."

They kissed again, and he took off.

CHAPTER 8

"This is a beautiful piece of land," Clara said, popping the last bite of her sandwich into her mouth. She crumpled the paper wrapper and disposed of it in the bag from the sandwich shop that sat on the console between them.

She surveyed the rolling fields, now dormant, that stretched to a line of trees on the horizon. "I can see why you love being here. It's so tranquil."

"You should see it in the spring, when all these fields are planted and it's a rolling sea of the most vibrant green."

"I'd love to."

"I'll bring you back, if you really mean it."

Clara took his hand and squeezed it. "I do."

"And the fall. That run of trees," he pointed, "are beyond spectacular."

"Spring and fall, then. Plus—I think it's beautiful right now." She turned to the back window and pointed to a large split-level house behind them. "Is that your grandfather's farmhouse?"

Kurt shook his head. "That's on the farm, but it's much newer. The couple who bought the farm built it. My grandpa's old house is just over that ridge to your right."

"Is it close enough to walk?"

"Sure."

"Would we need to ford any streams or anything?"

"No. It's dry land all the way. There's even a little track to follow. I park here whenever I come out and I usually walk over to see the house."

Clara zipped her jacket and reached for the door handle. "Let's go."

"It's not much to see. It's just a modest, three-bedroom house."

"With memories so dear to you that you visit it every time you're here." She opened her door. "Come on. Show me."

Kurt took her hand and led her to a narrow dirt path that traced a line between a stand of trees and a narrow creek, its surface crusted with ice.

"The bare branches of the trees look like lace against the blue sky," Clara said. "They're almost… architectural."

Kurt nodded and kept walking.

"Is this the creek you used to play in?"

"Yep. I know every inch of it, from the house to where we were parked. It looks tame now, but it'll double in size during the spring runoff. My grandmother was always scared to death that I'd drown in that creek."

"I can see why," Clara said.

"Nah—I was fine. Only fell in a couple of times."

They climbed the ridge on the hard-packed path until they reached the crest.

Clara stopped suddenly.

A simple two-story clapboard house with a gabled roof and wrap-around porch was nestled under the protective branches of a giant oak. A generous lawn staked out its territory from the woods. Identical sets of windows on the second floor reflected the sun and blue skies. The house needed paint, and the roof required attention, but the first impression of the place was one of permanence and durability, comfort and grace.

"Oh, Kurt. This is lovely!" She turned to him. "Why in the world didn't the owners want to live here?"

"My grandparents never put in a driveway—it was too expensive to grade one, with the creek and all. They just walked down the ridge to a barn where they parked their pickup truck. The new people didn't want to do that." He kissed the tip of her nose, which was shiny and red in the cold. "You're freezing. Let's get you back."

Clara pulled her hood over her ears and walked toward the house. "Can we look in the windows? No one lives here, right? We're not trespassing or anything."

"We are trespassing, but I don't think anyone lives here. I check the doors and windows every time I come." He shrugged. "I just want it to be locked up."

They climbed the three steps onto the front porch. Clara pressed her face to the window on the left side of the door.

"That's the living room," Kurt said.

"Look at that stone fireplace! I'll bet those are all hand-laid."

"By my grandfather," Kurt said with unmistakable pride.

"Is that water damage on the floor?"

Kurt pressed his face to the glass next to hers. "I think that could be sanded and fixed." He checked that the window was locked, and they made their way around the house.

"Someone would definitely want to remodel the kitchen," Clara said as they retraced their steps to the front of the house.

"I know exactly what I'd do with it," he said.

Clara grabbed his elbow. "Why don't you buy this place?"

"I don't want to live out here. I need to be close to my office."

"I'll bet they'd be thrilled to sell this to you. They're clearly not maintaining it. It must be an unwelcome expense."

"Like I said, why would I want it? Without a garage, it won't work as a fix-and-flip for me."

"You don't want to sell this to someone else. You should buy this for your weekend retreat... a second home."

Kurt stopped short. "I'd never thought of that. Second homes usually aren't within half an hour of your first home."

"So what? It feels like you've entered a whole new world out here. Being so close is a tremendous advantage."

Kurt stood on the porch, surveying the scene in front of him that he loved so much. "Clara Conway—you are a genius. I'm going to sleep on it overnight, but I think I'll find this new owner and make an offer."

Clara clasped her hands together in delight.

He turned to her and swept her off her feet. She shrieked as he swung her in a circle.

"Now—let's head back to my place. I know it's a day late, but I still owe you a Valentine's Day dinner." Kurt took her hand and they stepped off the porch.

"I'd love that. As I said, this will be a first—having a man cook dinner for me."

"I should warn you, I don't have a vast repertoire. Still, it should be good. I learned all the recipes from Maisie."

"In that case, I'm sure it'll be fabulous." They swung their hands as they walked. "And it wouldn't matter if it wasn't. The fact that you're making the effort means the world to me."

Kurt leaned in and kissed her.

"If we keep this up, we'll never get out of here," Clara said when they finally broke apart. "Race you," she said, sprinting to the car with Kurt in hot pursuit.

CHAPTER 9

"Stop, Maisie. Put that down." Joan took the half-full bag of sugar from the older woman and carried it to the counter. "It's too heavy for you."

"That couldn't have weighed more than twenty pounds," Maisie grumbled. "I've been lifting forty-pound bags of flour and sugar my whole life."

"Until you... had your..." Joan trailed off at the storm clouds gathering on Maisie's face.

"And I can still lift them. I'm recovered fully. My doctor's cleared me to go back to my regular activities." She glowered at Joan.

Four members of the bakery staff stopped rolling croissants for the next day's production and watched the interaction between the two women.

"We don't want you to tax yourself."

"Then what do you suggest I do around here?"

"We've got that nice chair for you behind the counter," Clara interjected. "You can keep an eye on the front of the store."

"So I'm supposed to sit in the corner all day, every day, and smile at customers?"

"You ring up sales, too," Clara said in a conciliatory voice.

"That's only if one of you doesn't beat me to the register." Maisie put her hand on her hip. "I'm not some hothouse plant, you know. You shouldn't leave me on the shelf. I can carry my weight around here."

"We know that," Joan said. "It's just that... we promised—"

Maisie cut her off. "You promised that husband of mine that you wouldn't let me work." Her voice rose an octave. "Let me tell you something—a hard day's work never hurt anyone." She walked to the worktable. "I'll help finish the croissants."

The four bakers resumed their task. "This is the last batch," one of them said. "We'll finish this in a few minutes."

Maisie threw her hands in the air and looked around herself. "We're not busy at the counter this afternoon. It looks like there really isn't anything for me to do. I'm not going to hang around here, sitting in that chair."

"Why don't you head home? Put your feet up." Joan said.

Maisie huffed. "You didn't hear a thing I just said, did you?"

Clara took Maisie's elbow and pulled her aside. "Nobody's trying to upset you," she whispered. "We haven't had our grand opening yet and we're not that busy. I overheard the bakers chatting yesterday. They're worried that I might have to lay someone off."

Maisie's expression did an about-face. "I'm so sorry to hear that. We never laid people off at the diner. I know how scary the prospect of losing your job is." She looked at Clara. "Have you reassured them?"

"I've tried."

"Do they think that if I take on more of the daily work, you'll lay one of them off?"

Clara shrugged. "Hard to say. I know they're nervous about us being overstaffed."

Maisie released a slow breath. "I don't want to cause anyone to lose their job." She glanced at Clara. "I need something to do. Kurt and I were talking about this recently." She pursed her lips. "I'll stay away from here if you think it will calm our bakers down."

"That should help, at least until business picks up." Clara patted Maisie's hand. "What will you do—since you're not a hothouse plant?" She grinned at her business partner.

"I'll go to the diner in the morning to see what I can do there. Maybe I'll work on the books. Josef hates doing that."

"Do you like bookkeeping?" Clara asked.

Maisie picked up her purse and headed for the door. "I loathe it. But it's better than sitting around, twiddling my thumbs."

Maisie followed Josef to his car the next morning.

"Do you want me to give you a lift to Sweets & Treats?"

He peered over the top of his glasses at his wife. "Aren't you feeling well enough to drive?"

"I'm perfectly fine. Everyone should stop asking me how I feel. I'm coming to the diner today—with you."

"Oh, okay." Josef opened her car door for her. "Can I ask why?"

"We're slow at the bakery and there's nothing for me to do. I thought I'd make myself useful at the diner." Maisie buckled her seat belt and swiveled to her husband. "Do you have any objection?"

"No. Of course not. It's just that—"

"I can't sit in that house one more minute." Maisie settled against her seat back. "Just drive. Please."

Josef shifted the car into gear. They made the quick trip to the diner in silence.

"The breakfast crew will already have coffee brewing and bacon on the grill," Josef said as he pulled into his parking spot.

"I thought I'd tackle the paperwork—posting invoices and receipts. You hate doing that. Your desk is usually an unholy mess."

He cleared his throat. "I've made a concerted effort to do better with that. We're all caught up."

"Then I'll work the hostess stand."

They got out of the car and proceeded toward the employee entrance.

He pointed to a small red Honda. "Our morning hostess is already here. We won't need two." His tone grew stern. "And you're not waiting—or bussing—tables."

Maisie stopped abruptly. "Then I'll do something else.

I'm losing my mind, Josef. I've got to find a way to occupy my time."

He turned to her and pulled her into his arms, resting his chin on the top of her head. "I know you do, Maisie. There's got to be something you can turn your considerable talents to. I'm not sure there's anything worthy of you at the diner."

She nodded her head against his chest.

"I hoped that a part ownership in Sweets & Treats would be your new chapter. Maybe it still will be once it's up and running," he said.

"I did too, but not anymore. Clara has it all well in hand. I don't want to barge in on her dream. She deserves to do this on her own," she whispered.

"I'm sorry, sweetheart," Josef said.

Maisie pulled back and smiled at him. "It's my job to figure out what I want to do when I grow up. This pity party is now officially over."

Josef leaned down and kissed her. "You're still the bravest person I've ever known."

Maisie flushed. "We can't stand out here, necking in the parking lot. What will our employees think? Let's get to work. I'm sure I'll figure out my next act soon."

CHAPTER 10

*C*lara stretched her slippered feet out on the rug in front of her, raised her arms high over her head, and stretched.

Noelle jumped onto the sofa next to Clara. She pawed her mistress's thigh before jumping back to the rug. Noelle turned in a circle, glanced back at Clara, then ran to the back door and scratched the frame.

"Okay, girl. I get it. You have to go out."

Clara heaved herself off the sofa and followed her dog. "You're awfully feisty this morning. No one would ever guess you'd had a tooth pulled on Wednesday." She opened the kitchen door and Noelle shot down the steps to her favorite spot for doing her business.

Clara pulled her robe around her and stepped onto the stoop. The sun was high and bright in an azure sky, and a gentle breeze carried the first hint of spring. Despite the cool temperature, she felt warm in the sun.

She shielded her eyes with her hand and scanned the bushes leaning against the fence surrounding her small backyard, searching for the beginnings of new growth. The bushes were gray and barren, but something was trying to poke its head up through brambles to her left.

Clara skipped down the steps and went straight to the spot, her slippers crunching on the dormant grass. She loved spring flowers that grew from bulbs. Hyacinths, tulips, crocus—all were wonderful—but her favorite was the daffodil. She squatted and examined the growth. The shoots making their way to the light were unmistakably daffodils.

Clara clasped her hands. She hoped there might be other bulbs planted there. Tabitha Trent, her elderly land-lady, had kept a legendary garden here before age and arthritis had curtailed her efforts. When left on their own, bulbs multiplied and kept coming up year after year. She was excited to see what would emerge from her dormant garden this spring.

Clara turned to continue her examination of the garden when she spotted Noelle along the fence at the far end of the yard. Her terrier mix had her snout to the ground, hindquarters in the air, as her front paws dug furiously at a spot along the fence.

"Noelle." Clara cried. "Stop that!"

Dirt flew over Noelle's back haunches as she continued to dig.

"Noelle!" Clara began running across the yard. "Stop that. NOW."

Noelle glanced at Clara, but kept digging.

Clara lunged for Noelle's collar and pulled her back.

"What in the world do you think you're doing?" Clara lost her balance and sat on the grass, pulling Noelle onto her lap.

"You just had surgery—you're supposed to be taking it easy." She wiped dirt off of Noelle's muzzle and gently opened her mouth, examining the area on the upper gum where the tooth had been extracted. "All right—it looks okay to me." She held Noelle's muzzle and looked into her eyes. "What were you doing? You don't want to dig your way out of our yard!"

Noelle thumped her tail against Clara's leg.

"Look at these muddy paws. Let's get you inside and cleaned up."

Noelle hopped off of Clara's lap as Clara got to her feet. She took a step back to the spot at the fence where she'd been digging.

"Don't even think about it," Clara said.

Noelle nodded as if she understood, and followed Clara across the yard and into the house.

Clara had just finished cleaning Noelle's paws when Kurt called.

"Hey, beautiful. I'm calling to check on my girls. How's everyone doing?"

Clara dumped the last muddy towels into the washer and padded into the living room. "We're fine. Noelle's recovered from her tooth extraction like it never happened. She's back to wolfing down her food and acting like she has cabin fever. I know she's ready for a long walk this afternoon. Meanwhile, I'm more grateful than I can say for a lazy Sunday."

"I was glad to get your text that the inspectors signed off on the installation of the bakery equipment at the patisserie. Does that mean you're ready to handle all the baking from Sweets & Treats?"

"It does. There's nothing left at the old bakery building behind the diner. But I'm not sure the current layout will be as efficient as I thought. I started moving stuff around yesterday afternoon."

"Wait a minute—some of those mixers are extremely heavy. You weren't doing this on your own, were you?"

Clara remained silent a beat too long as she rubbed her sore lower back.

"Why didn't you call me? I would have come over to help you."

"You've been busier than I have, with your trial and the purchase of your grandparent's old farmhouse. Did you get the keys?"

"Yesterday."

"Happy to hear that."

"In fact, that's why I'm calling. I thought I'd go out there this afternoon and take a look inside. I wondered if you'd want to go with me?"

"You know I would! I'm dying to see the inside."

"We can take Noelle with us and kill two birds with one stone. She'll love it out there. The weather is supposed to be beautiful today."

"After what she's been through, she deserves an adventure. There's a major winter storm bearing down on us tomorrow. Some forecasts are calling it a blizzard. We're all going to be cooped up inside for a while. It would do me good to be out in the fresh air, too. I've holed up in one bakery building or the other from before dawn until after dusk for the past two weeks."

"I want to stop at the hardware store to pick up a

lockbox for the new house. Workers will need access. I'll do that and pick you up in thirty minutes?"

"I haven't even showered yet. Can you give me an hour?"

"You don't need to curl your hair or slap on makeup for me. You're always the prettiest woman in the room."

Clara flushed. She didn't agree, but she loved that he felt this way.

"Have you eaten?"

"No. I've just had my coffee."

"After the hardware store, I'll pick up brunch and we can eat at your place before we head out. I'll read the paper while you finish getting ready. You were just saying that you were looking forward to a relaxed day. I don't want to rush you. We've got all day."

They ended their call.

"We're spending our day with Kurt, Noelle. What do you think about that?"

Noelle uttered a short woof and trotted toward the bathroom.

Clara smiled and shook her head. That smart dog of hers had understood every word of their conversation— she was sure of it.

CHAPTER 11

"That must be Ian," Clara said. "No one else knocks on my door." She shoved the empty Styrofoam container from her breakfast into the trash and headed to answer it.

Noelle rose from her spot under the tiny breakfast table and looked up at Kurt, her tail wagging at warp speed and her eyes hopeful.

Kurt held the last bite of his meal between his fingers: a perfectly crisp piece of thick-cut bacon. He brought it to his mouth and stopped, looking into her pleading expression. "You've had a hard week, haven't you, girl? I think you've earned this."

He lowered his hand, and she snatched the bacon in one swift motion.

"Don't tell your mother. I'll get in trouble."

Noelle licked the evidence from her lips as Clara and Ian entered the kitchen.

"Ian's come down to take Noelle for a long walk," Clara said.

"My mom said we should enjoy the day before the storm."

"That's what we're going to do." Kurt rose and disposed of his trash.

"She just got back from the pharmacy. My great-grandmother's getting a cold and she wanted to have her asthma meds and OTC stuff on hand. Mom said the drugstore was packed and the grocery next door was a madhouse. She picked up extra water, milk, and bread. She said to tell you they were selling out of stuff, in case you need to stock up."

Kurt looked at Clara. "I'm fine, but do you need anything? Maybe we should do that instead of checking my new property."

"I'll bring home supplies from the patisserie," Clara said. "If it gets as bad as they're predicting, I may not be able to open it—and if I do open—I won't have many customers. I'll use what I have. I don't want to spend this beautiful day inside a crowded store with frenzied customers."

"I can't argue with that," Kurt said. He turned to Ian. "We're taking Noelle with us to visit a house I just bought outside of town. Would you like to come with us?"

Ian looked between them. "Are you sure it's okay?"

"Definitely," Clara said. "It's a beautiful setting. We'll be busy inside the house, assessing its condition. We wouldn't let Noelle explore unsupervised, so she'd be cooped up with us. She'll be much happier running around outside with you."

"There's a creek by the house and everything," Kurt said. "It was my grandparent's house. I spent some of the happiest days of my childhood there."

"Sounds great. I'll go tell my mom."

"We'll meet you at Kurt's Jeep. Tell Laura you'll be home by late afternoon."

Ian bounded out the door, Noelle in hot pursuit.

KURT AND CLARA picked their way through the mass of brambles and weeds to the house nestled at the top of the hill.

Ian and Noelle scampered ahead of them, unhindered by the difficult terrain.

"The first thing I need to do is have someone come in and clear this lawn. I wish I'd have thought of it last week. With the snow coming in, it'll have to wait."

"You'll need a machete to get in here once things start to grow again."

"I've hired an engineer to see about a driveway from the road. I can't park on the berm and walk up here for the rest of my life. A garage around back is part of my plan." He pointed to the right of the house, where Ian and Noelle had just disappeared.

"They're having a grand time," Clara said. "She'll sleep well tonight. I hope this isn't too much for her."

"Don't worry. She'll stop if she gets tired. Dogs are much more sensible than people. And Ian will take good care of her."

They climbed the steps to the porch.

Kurt held up the key. "Here goes." He inserted it in the lock and tried to turn it. The key wouldn't budge.

"Oh, gosh." Clara sighed.

"It's an old lock." Kurt pursed his lips and began jiggling

the key back and forth, pulling up on the handle. One tumbler fell, and then another. The lock clicked, and the door swung open on creaky hinges.

"Add 'lubricate lock and hinges' to my to-do list," Kurt said as he held the door open. "After you."

Clara stepped inside.

The interior was damp and chilly. Wallpaper that had once been pretty was now water stained and peeling. Unmistakable evidence of rodent infestation was visible along the baseboards. A section of the wooden flooring buckled by the stairs.

Kurt sucked in a breath. "I told myself it would be in rough shape. Rewiring and re-plumbing—taking it back to the studs—would be essential. I've budgeted for a new roof, too." He turned in a slow circle. "That all sounds good —on paper. It's daunting when you actually see how bad it is."

Clara walked to him and took his arm, drawing him with her to the living room window. Full of cobwebs and coated with grime, the large glass panes flooded a wide swath of the honey-colored floor with sunshine. "Close your eyes," she said.

Kurt complied.

"Now, think of a wonderful memory from your child-hood. In this very spot." She watched the lines creasing his forehead ease as he conjured the happy image.

"Okay. When you open your eyes, I want you to see that image. Not the dust and debris that you'll clear out of here. Replace your second thoughts and regrets with happy images from the past. And imagine the good times ahead. Memorize that feeling, and we'll go through the rest of the house. You'll lock this door when we're done with double the excitement you had for this house when we started out this morning."

Kurt opened his eyes and saw the living room of his youth. "You're right—I can visualize this house as I want it to be." He turned to her and pulled her into a tight hug. "I'm so thankful you're here," he whispered in her ear.

She planted a kiss on his cheek and stepped back. "I can't wait to see the rest of this place. Lead on!"

They compared notes when they'd concluded their examination of the first floor.

"I like your idea of combining the kitchen and dining room into a large, eat-in kitchen," Kurt said. "I'm never going to need a formal dining room."

"Exactly," Clara said. "You'd want to tape out the dimensions of the cabinets and island on the floor, but I think you'll have room to sandwich in a small powder room on the other side of the stairs."

"Definitely. I don't know how my grandparents survived with only an upstairs bathroom."

"I bet they never had to go to the gym. Their daily lives provided all the exercise they needed."

"I cringe when I realize they stayed here until they died —at eighty-nine and ninety-one."

"It's wonderful that they lived such long lives, in a home they cherished." Clara walked to the large window over the sink and admired the view. She stepped to her left and mimicked chopping vegetables and kneading dough. "I'd keep the sink right here. This will be the most peaceful place to do food prep."

Kurt came up behind her and circled her with his arms.

"There used to be a beautiful lilac bush along the tree line."

"And I didn't think this could be more perfect." Clara leaned against him and they gazed into the backyard as Noelle zoomed into view, with Ian chasing her.

Kurt chuckled. "Looks like they're having a good time."

Noelle exited the scene, then appeared from the opposite direction, turning back to Ian and crouching down on her front paws, her tail held high.

"She's playing catch me if you can," Clara said.

Ian raced into view, panting.

"He's trying, but he's no match for her," Kurt said. "Should we go rescue them?"

"I haven't seen the upstairs yet," Clara protested.

"It's three bedrooms and a minuscule bathroom. It didn't even have a shower—just a tub."

"Then it'll only take a minute. I want to go up there." She wriggled out of his embrace. "Show me."

"All right. I'm going first on the stairs, in case they're not safe," Kurt said.

"Fine by me."

The stairs were sturdy and didn't even squeak as they climbed to the small landing. The door at the top of the stairs led to a bathroom that was, indeed, minuscule. Two tiny bedrooms opened off the hall on the left and one small bedroom stood on the right.

"Look at these lovely baseboards and wooden doors. They're still in remarkably good shape. The glass door knobs must be original and they're all here." She fingered the facets on one of the knobs. "You'd spend a fortune replacing these."

Kurt led her into the largest bedroom and pointed to

the ceiling. "I helped my grandfather install the crown molding in here. This wasn't prefabricated molding, like you'd buy today. He was a talented woodworker and made it in the barn one winter. He kept it a secret from my grandmother, and we installed it for her birthday. I still remember how thrilled she was. Said it made her feel so fancy."

"That's the sweetest story."

"My grandparents were true soul mates. They met when they were in elementary school and married right out of high school. You'd think they'd have taken each other for granted, but that never happened. They were sweethearts their whole lives. I don't think the spark ever died for them."

Clara blinked rapidly as she cleared her throat. "They sound like the most amazing couple." She walked around the room, chin tilted up, admiring the molding. "This is incredibly special. I'm so glad you bought this house."

"Me too. I've had nightmares for years that I'd drive out here one day to find someone had torn the house down to make way for a utilitarian storage shed."

"That would've been a travesty," Clara said.

Kurt checked the lock on the bedroom window. He pointed to the front yard below, where Ian and Noelle were slowly making their way to the front porch. "It looks like she's finally run out of steam."

Clara checked her watch. "We'd better get them home. Are you happy with your purchase?" she asked as they descended the stairs.

"To be honest," Kurt said. "It was touch and go when we first walked in. I expected it would be this bad, but seeing it is another thing." He looked over his shoulder at her. "What you did when we came in—when you had me close my eyes and refocus—changed everything. Thank you for helping me… keep my vision for this place."

"That's what partners do," Clara replied as they stepped onto the porch.

Kurt's chin came up sharply.

"I mean… what friends are for," she quickly amended, dropping to one knee to pat Noelle. "Hey, Ian," she said. "Looks like the two of you tuckered yourselves out."

"We sure did. That dog can run for miles. I'd swear she knows this place. It was like she's been here before."

"That's possible," Clara said. "She was a stray. We never found her owners."

Kurt finished installing the lockbox on the front door. He inserted his key, set the code, and shut the compartment. "I guess she could be from around here. We're only about seven miles from town."

"Feels like we're in another world," Ian said.

"Well… whether or not she used to live out here, she's mine now." Clara picked up her beloved companion and planted kisses on her neck. "She's coming home with me. We'd better be on our way."

Ian moved off toward the Jeep.

"You're going to carry her?"

Clara nodded. "I think she overdid it, racing around out here."

Kurt smiled and scooped Noelle out of Clara's arms. "I'll carry her for you."

"Thank you," Clara replied.

Kurt held her gaze. "That's what partners do."

"You're sure you're feeling better?" Laura Ramsey set the morning newspaper and an insulated cup containing tea on the end table. She peered anxiously at her grandmother, ensconced in her chair by the bay window on the front of the gracious Victorian house.

"My meds are kicking in, and I'm feeling much better this morning." Tabitha pointed to the array of prescription bottles and her inhaler lined up on the table. "You've given me everything I'll need, right here. I've got my book and my knitting—and now my tea. I'll be fine."

"I made tuna salad for Ian's lunch. There's a sandwich for you in the fridge."

"Splendid. You take such good care of me, honey. I'll spend my day right here, in my favorite chair. It's going to be a beautiful morning—like yesterday. I can't believe we're supposed to have a snowstorm this afternoon. Maybe it'll miss us."

"The weather report says it'll be here late this afternoon

—just in time for the evening commute. I'll come home as soon as school gets out. I don't want to get caught up in traffic."

"You'd better get going, dear." Tabitha looked at her ancient wristwatch. "It's after seven."

Ian appeared in the doorway, stuffing his arms into his down jacket. " 'Morning, Gran," he said to his great-grandmother. "I'm ready."

"Have a good day, you two."

Laura leaned over and kissed her grandmother's forehead. "You feel warm. I should take your temperature."

"You'll do no such thing. That'll make you late. I'm perfectly fine."

Laura stepped back. "You don't look flushed." Her brows knitted. "Call me if you need anything." She tapped the cell phone on the table.

Tabitha rolled her eyes, but nodded.

"I don't have practice after school today," Ian said. "They canceled it because of the storm. I'll be home by three. I'll check on you as soon as I get here."

"Don't worry about me—I'm right as rain." Tabitha settled back into her chair and picked up the newspaper. "Now get going. I want to catch up on the news." She pulled a pen from the pocket of her cardigan. "And I intend to do the crossword—in ink."

~

"Come on, Noelle," Clara called from the kitchen door. "Mommy's running late."

The terrier dutifully trotted up the steps and into the house.

Clara shut the door with her hip as she wound her luxurious new sapphire-colored scarf around her neck. "I'll be home early. We probably won't have many customers. Everyone's getting ready for the storm."

Noelle sat at her mistress's feet and wagged her tail.

"I know it looks beautiful right now—just like yesterday. That's all supposed to change this afternoon." Clara bent over and kissed the top of Noelle's head. "I may be home with you for a couple of days. We'll have plenty of time to cuddle then. See you soon." Clara set out for work.

Later that afternoon, Clara sank into a bistro chair at the table by the front display window of Sweets & Treats.

Joan sat down opposite her.

The two women locked eyes.

"I don't know about you," Clara said, "but I'm shell-shocked."

Joan nodded her agreement. "This is the first time since we opened at seven that we haven't had a customer in the shop."

"We haven't even officially opened yet," Clara said. "If our grand opening is as busy as this, I'll be thrilled."

"I think people were panic-buying due to the storm," Joan replied.

"Stocking up on croissants and cookies, eclairs, and cakes? They're hardly essentials."

"If I'm going to be stuck inside, I'll want those." Joan looked at the display cases around them. "As a matter of fact, we're going to sell out. We put everything we had in the cases right after lunch. I saved a box of goodies to take home for my family. Should I put them in the cases instead? I'm sure we'll sell them."

"You'll do no such thing. You deserve those treats." Clara checked the time on her phone. "It's almost three. We may be done for the day." She pointed to the front window. "The weather has turned. The sun's behind those clouds moving in. I'll bet people will head for home soon."

Joan opened the weather app on her phone. "This shows snow starting before five. Winds are picking up…" She was interrupted as a sudden gust rattled the door. "Now."

The signboard on the sidewalk blew over with a sharp thwap.

Joan rose. "I'll bring the sign in."

"I'm going to send the staff home. They should be finished cleaning the equipment by now. We're not going to bake anything else today. I can handle any customers that trickle in," Clara said. "I'll close and head home by four."

"They'll appreciate that. Everyone has either kids—or aging relatives—to see to. All this talk of the storm of the century is making the whole town nervous."

"You can go, too. I'll manage on my own."

"I'd like to head out by four, but I can stay until then. If we're not busy, I'd like to show you how I'd rearrange a few things in the bakery."

"You're all stocked up at home?"

"Absolutely. I'm not a last-minute kind of gal. Jerry will be home and have dinner waiting for me." Joan smiled coyly. "To tell you the truth, we're looking forward to being snowed in."

Clara raised an eyebrow and grinned. "I'm happy to hear it."

"Bring in the sign and I'll meet you in back. The bell over the door will alert us to any customers." Clara pushed herself to her feet. "I'll tell the staff to be on their way."

CHAPTER 13

Ian bounded up the back steps and pulled at the kitchen door, tugging hard to open it against the stiff breeze. He dropped his backpack by the door and raced into the living room. "I'm home, Gran…" His voice trailed off as he regarded his beloved great-grandmother.

She was sunk back into her chair, her head to one side, sound asleep.

He tiptoed to her and picked up her insulated mug. He always made her a fresh cuppa when he got home from school. It surprised Ian that it felt full. She always drank her tea.

He paused and looked at her. Her chest rose and fell, but with an unmistakable rattle. The newspaper lay on her lap, folded back to the crossword. Tabitha had only completed a few words.

Ian bit his lip. She prided herself on working the crossword straight through. When he took the mug to the kitchen and put the kettle on, he opened the fridge to get the cream she took in her tea. He saw that the tuna sandwich his mother had left for Tabitha's lunch remained untouched.

Ian slammed the fridge shut and dug his cell phone out of his backpack. He placed a call to his mother.

Laura answered on the first ring. "You're home?"

"Mom—grandma's not right."

"What do you mean?" Laura shouted into the phone as she walked into the wind on her way to her car.

"She's asleep—I think she's been that way all day. She didn't eat her lunch—and she didn't finish the crossword."

"Her medication can make her sleepy," Laura said, pushing down a rising tide of panic.

"There's more. Her breathing rattles. You always told me that's bad."

Laura yanked open her car door and flung herself into the driver's seat. "I'm on my way. Stay with her until I get there."

"Okay. Should I wake her?"

"No. As long as she's breathing, she's okay. If it becomes labored, do you remember how to give her a blast from her inhaler?"

"I do."

"I'll be home in ten minutes," Laura said. "I'll stay on the phone with you until I get there. Go back into the living room with her. I'm putting you on speaker. Can you hear me okay?"

"Yes." The tea kettle whistled. Ian turned it off and went back to his great-grandmother.

"She's still the same."

"I'm going to take her to the emergency room when I

get home. If this storm is as bad as they say it's going to be, she'll be better off in the hospital."

"Okay," Ian said. "I haven't taken Noelle out yet. I came straight here to check on Gran."

"You can take care of her after we leave."

"Aren't I going with you?"

"I don't think that's a good idea. The hospital is probably going to be packed. You'll be more comfortable at home."

"What if you get stuck at the hospital?"

"Clara will be in the guest house. And I don't want to spend the night at the hospital. If they admit your great-grandmother, I'll come home."

"Maybe we should invite Clara and Noelle to spend the night at our house. We have a backup generator and our heater never goes out, even if we lose electricity. It seems safer if they're with us."

"That's a great idea. I'm pulling onto our street now. I'll call her after I see to Gran."

Laura pulled up to the back door and raced inside.

Tabitha stirred as Laura hurried to her side and placed a hand on her forehead.

"She's burning up." Laura knelt at Tabitha's feet and took one of her grandmother's hands into hers. "Can you hear me?"

Tabitha opened her eyes. Her expression was distant and unfocused.

"I think you're sick, Gran. Sounds like pneumonia —again."

Tabitha nodded and reached for her cane.

"Get her coat." Laura turned to Ian. "Bring my purse, too. Put all of her prescriptions in it. I'll take them with us."

Ian was back in a flash.

Together, they helped Tabitha get to her feet and put her coat on.

"Let's each take an arm and walk her to my car."

"Gran weighs nothing, Mom. I can carry her." Ian swept the fragile old woman into his arms.

Laura smiled at her son. She sometimes forgot that he was a young man. And a very sensible, capable one at that.

Laura led the way, opening the back passenger door. "She'll be more comfortable here."

Ian laid Tabitha on the back seat and gently secured a seat belt.

"Thank you, Ian," Laura said as she got behind the wheel and rolled down her window. "Don't worry. They'll take good care of her. I'll call Clara as soon as I can."

Ian nodded. "Is it okay if I take Noelle for a walk?"

"If you stay on our street. The storm's definitely moving in. You don't want to get caught out in it."

"I know that. We'll stay close."

Laura patted his arm, started the car, and headed for the emergency room.

CHAPTER 14

Ian watched his mother's car until it turned right at the corner and was lost from view. His great-grandmother had had pneumonia before. She would be fine.

A gust of wind blew open his unzipped jacket and stung the tips of his ears. It was noticeably colder than when he'd gotten off the school bus at the corner, not thirty minutes ago. Large, heavy wet snowflakes had begun to fall.

He went back into the house, headed straight to the coat closet, and pulled a cardboard box off the top shelf, labeled "Winter Gear" in his mother's neat block letters. He brought the box to the kitchen table and foraged until he found the thermal scarf, hat, and gloves she'd bought him the prior Christmas when he'd gone snow camping with his Boy Scout troop. They'd learned all sorts of interesting things about surviving in a snowstorm. Things he'd hoped he'd never need to know, but were still interesting.

Like wearing layers. He had on a T-shirt and sweater under his jacket. That counted as layers. And to carry a flashlight. He rummaged through the box until he found his small LED flashlight. Even though he wasn't going out in a blizzard—he was only going to walk Noelle—he slipped the flashlight into his pocket.

Take a cell phone. He patted the back pocket of his jeans. His phone was there.

What was the last thing? Ian paused, remembering what his scout master had told them. Water! Stay hydrated. Ian grabbed a bottle of water on his way through the kitchen.

He stepped outside, and the wind whipped his scarf back, almost tearing it from his neck. A thick blanket of clouds obliterated the sun. It would get dark earlier than usual. Snow was falling in heavy, wet flakes.

The path to the guest house was slick with a solid coating of snow. He doubted Noelle would be eager to come out in this weather. He'd let her do her business, feed her, and bring her to the main house to wait for word from his mother.

Ian put his key in the lock. For the second time in the past month, Noelle hadn't been watching for him at the window or barking at the door.

He shoved the door open. "Noelle!" He went directly to the spot under Clara's bed where he'd found her when she'd been suffering from her abscessed tooth.

Noelle wasn't there—or anywhere else in the house. The kitchen door stood ajar, just wide enough to allow a Noelle-size dog to slip through the opening.

The latch on the door stuck. If it didn't catch, the door could blow open. He always made sure the door was securely locked when he left, but he hadn't come by that morning. Maybe Clara didn't know about the sticky latch. He swallowed hard and stepped into the backyard.

"Okay, Noelle..." The words froze in his mouth. She wasn't in the fenced yard. "NOELLE," he bellowed. He ran down the steps into the yard, looking around him for any sign of her.

Snow had accumulated in the shadow cast by the house. A paw-shaped indentation caught his eye.

Ian followed the trail of paw prints to the fence. He dropped to his knees to examine the fence. The chain-link was intact—Noelle couldn't have gotten through it.

A mound of dirt, rapidly being buried by the snow, sat at the base of the fence.

Ian pulled off his glove with his teeth and stuck his hand into an indentation behind the dirt. He pushed his hand further and his fingertips came up on the other side of the fence. Noelle had dug herself out of the yard.

Snow continued to come down hard. The wind howled around him. It would soon be dark.

Ian leaned over the fence. He could still make out the trail of paw prints, but they would soon be covered with fresh snow.

He looked at the open kitchen door. Noelle couldn't have gone far. He didn't want to waste time going back to close the door or leave a note. If he waited even a few minutes, she'd be farther away and he might never find her. He'd be back before anyone would find a note, anyway.

Ian shoved his hand back into his glove. He inserted the toe of his right boot into the fence and hoisted himself up and over. The toe of his left boot slipped out of position and he slid down the far side of the fence.

The back pocket of his jeans snagged on a sharp corner of the chain-link. Ian lurched backward when he hit the ground, tearing himself free. He didn't notice his cell phone tumble into the brambles.

Ian got quickly to his feet, switched on the flashlight he was now happy he'd brought with him, and trained it on Noelle's paw prints. They led into the wooded gully that ran between the backyards on his side of the street and the street behind it.

"Noelle!" The wind carried his voice behind him. He bent over, keeping his eyes on the rapidly disappearing paw prints, and set out on his desperate search.

CHAPTER 15

"Oh, my gosh, look at the time," Joan exclaimed as she glanced at her cell phone, sitting on the worktable. "It's after four."

"Holy cow. I would have said it wasn't even three yet. The way we re-arranged the bread baking area should improve workflow a lot," Clara said. "We can tweak anything else later. You need to get out of here."

Joan walked to the solid metal rear door and poked her head out. "It's really coming down. There's an inch on the ground already."

Clara opened one of the refrigerators and took out a tray of two dozen eggs. "Here," she placed them on top of Joan's bakery box of treats. "Take these, too. You live way out in the country. You may get stranded."

Joan hesitated, then smiled. "You could be right. Thank you." She stuffed her arms into her jacket. "I'll wait for you."

"No—you won't. I live less than a mile from here. I'm

going to load some groceries into my car and be on my way."

Joan picked up her packages and reached for the door. "You promise me you won't get carried away in here?"

"I promise. I love this patisserie, but I don't want to get snowed in here. I'll be five minutes behind you."

"Okay," Joan pushed open the door.

"Drive safely," Clara said as Joan disappeared into the storm.

Clara stacked a tray of eggs, a two-pound block of butter, a large bag of ground coffee, and two loaves of artisan bread on the worktable by the door. She checked the lock on the front door and had just finished ferrying her supplies to her car when she felt her phone vibrate in her purse.

She fished her phone out of her purse and answered it, holding it to her ear with her shoulder.

"Clara," Laura raised her voice to be heard over the chatter and blaring PA system in the emergency department waiting room.

Clara stowed the remaining items in the back of her SUV and slammed the hatch shut. She slipped on the snow as she made her way along the side of the car. "Laura," she said, tugging her door open and throwing herself inside, out of the storm. "Where are you?"

"I'm at the hospital."

"Oh, no! Is it…"

"Tabitha? Yes. I'm fairly certain she has pneumonia again. I brought her in about an hour ago. They just took her back for X-rays."

"I'm so sorry, but I'm glad she's at the hospital. This storm is no joke. I can't believe how quickly the weather changed."

"I heard someone in the waiting room say that we've had two inches in the last hour. And it's getting worse."

"I can believe it." Clara looked out of her windshield at the snow coming down. "I don't think I've ever seen anything like this."

"Are you home?" Laura asked.

"I'm sitting in my car at the patisserie. I'll start driving as soon as we hang up. You shouldn't try to come home from the hospital," Clara said. "Will they let you stay with Tabitha?"

"I think so, but I hadn't planned to."

"You may not have a choice. Don't worry about Ian. I'll fix him dinner—and breakfast. He can stay in the guest house with me, if he wants."

"He suggested that you and Noelle come up to the main house to stay with us. Our heater is gas and won't go out if we lose electricity. The fireplace in the guest house heats the living room and kitchen, but the bedrooms get cold when the electricity goes out."

"That's a great idea. Thank you," Clara said. "I'll be there shortly and I'll have Ian help me bring some of my clothes and Noelle's food and medicines up to the house. We'll hunker down together. I'll bake shortbread for Tabitha— for whenever we can take it to her."

"This is such a relief, Clara. To have you there. I don't know what I'd do without you."

"You've been so kind to me," Clara replied. "I'm glad I

can return the favor. Don't worry about anything at home. Let us know when you get news about Tabitha."

"Drive safely," Laura said. "I'm supposed to turn my cell phone off once I leave this waiting room, so if I don't answer, text me."

"Will do. I'm praying for you both."

CHAPTER 16

Ian lurched across the uneven terrain. He kept his head lowered, his flashlight searching for the paw prints that were now almost obliterated by the heavy curtain of fresh snow. Despite the frigid air, the hair at the nape of his neck was damp with perspiration.

"Noelle!" he bellowed again, knowing that his words were drowned out by the howling wind.

He stumbled and his right knee crashed against an outcropping of rock. Ian righted himself and turned in a tight circle. He could barely make out the trees ten feet in front of him, let alone the houses that he knew would be on either side of the gully. He reached for his phone in his back pocket. It was time to call for help.

His pocket was empty, the fabric torn free on one side. He'd lost his phone. Panic tasted like acid in his mouth. Noelle wouldn't survive in this much longer. He didn't think he would, either. He should go back. Ian swiveled his head one way and then the other. He couldn't tell which way he'd come from. He'd been walking into the wind, but the way the storm howled, it seemed like every direction put him walking into the wind.

He trained his flashlight on the ground around him. All traces of paw prints were gone. His eyes stung with unshed tears. He wasn't going to find Noelle. The best thing he could do was continue walking in this residential area. He'd eventually run into a house. Or a road.

Ian remembered the water bottle in his pocket and realized he was thirsty. He pulled out the bottle, took a long drink of the ice-cold liquid, and resumed walking.

He'd trudged on for another five long minutes when his feet flew out from under him and he landed, hard, on his back. Ian lay in a daze, the wind knocked out of him. He brought his gloved hand to his cheek to brush away something wet.

Noelle rested her front paws on his chest and licked his face.

His hand connected with her furry coat, crusted with snow. Ian pushed himself into a sitting position and drew the dog into a tight hug. His tears of gratitude mixed with her saliva and froze on his face.

He got to his feet, still holding her close. "Okay, girl. You'll be fine. We're going to find our way out of this —together."

He secured the small dog inside his oversize down jacket, her head jutting out at the collar under his chin.

Buoyed by his delight at finding Noelle, Ian turned his flashlight to the ground and made slow, steady progress forward.

CHAPTER 17

Clara's tires slipped on the road and her windshield wipers swung at top speed, barely able to assure visibility. She held the steering wheel in an iron grip. It took fifteen minutes to traverse the short distance to the house.

She held her breath when she turned into the driveway. The steep incline from the street to the house would be treacherous.

She tapped the accelerator, and the SUV inched forward until it reached level ground by the kitchen door. Clara blew out a breath and released her death grip on the steering wheel. She was home and wouldn't have to go out again until the storm was over.

Clara forced her way from the car to the house as the wind whipped her hair around her face. She rapped soundly on the kitchen door. Ian could help her unload the groceries. Then she'd move her car to her parking spot.

Clara waited, hugging herself and stamping her feet in the cold. He must not be able to hear her above the storm.

The kitchen light was on—he had to be home. She walked gingerly around the house to the front door, taking care not to lose her footing.

Clara rang the bell and waited. She rang it again. Maybe Ian was at the guest house with Noelle.

She proceeded slowly to the guest house, slipping and sliding on the snow-covered walkway. She could barely make out the living room light, dim even at close range. The front door was unlocked, and she was grateful to step out of the storm.

The frigid temperature inside and lack of greeting from her faithful companion instantly hit her like a slap in the face. Clara dropped her purse on the floor in the entryway and raced toward the racket at the back of the house. Her kitchen door was banging open and shut. Snow had accumulated inside the door.

Clara flipped on the back door light. It did little to penetrate the storm. She flung herself down the steps. "Noelle! Ian!" she screamed their names, over and over, while searching in the near white-out conditions.

What in the world had happened to them? Something was very wrong—and Clara needed help.

She returned to the house and frantically dug through her purse for her cell phone. Damn! She must have left it on the seat of her car. Clara fought her way through the storm back to her car. She flung herself inside, found her phone on the passenger seat, and placed her call.

Kurt picked it up on the fourth ring.

"Kurt," she wailed before he'd said a word.

"What's wrong?"

"Ian—and Noelle. They're missing!"

"What do you mean?"

"I just got home. They're supposed to be here, but they're not in the guest house or the main house."

"Maybe they're with Laura?" he suggested reasonably.

"She's at the hospital with Tabitha. She thinks her grandmother has pneumonia. Ian was supposed to be here with Noelle. And they're not."

"I just left Maisie and Josef's. I'll be there in a couple of minutes."

"Park on the street—the driveway is getting treacherous."

"I've got four-wheel drive and snow tires. I'll be fine. Don't panic. We'll find them."

Clara bit her lip as she stared at the snow pelting her windshield. Maybe Ian had taken Noelle for a walk and they'd stopped at a friend's house. He would have called Laura to let her know, and her phone was turned off. Surely that was it. She was feeling better when she remembered the unlocked door to the guest house and the back door standing open. Ian was far too responsible to have left her place in that state.

Clara didn't notice Kurt until his arm emerged from the darkness and knocked on the driver's side window. She hopped out of the car and slipped as her foot touched the ground.

Kurt reached out to steady her.

"Maybe he's with a friend," Kurt said.

Clara shook her head. She took his hand and pulled him with her to the guest house. "That occurred to me, but I don't think so. Wait until you see my house." Clara explained everything she'd seen and done.

"You've called his cell phone?"

"It goes to voice mail after five rings."

"He's probably contacted his mother, but she's not getting his message. She'll call you when she does."

"Who knows when that will be?" Clara's voice rose an octave. "I can't wait—my gut tells me they're in trouble."

Kurt rubbed his chin. "I have a buddy who's an ER physician. He should be on duty. I'll call to ask him to find Laura and have her call us."

"Thank you," Clara said, dabbing her runny nose with a tissue.

He placed the call and nodded in satisfaction when he was done. "Doc's working. He said he'll have someone locate Laura."

"What else can we do?"

"If we don't hear from Laura in the next fifteen minutes, I think we should call the police."

Clara's eyes filled with tears. How would anyone find them tonight, in this storm?

"Didn't you say something the other day about Noelle digging near the fence? I'm going to feel my way around the fence—see if there are any breaks where Noelle could have gotten out," Kurt said.

"Yes, maybe she's been at it again." Clara looked at him. "I covered up the spot she was digging before so she wouldn't get out."

"If she was in the yard this afternoon, she would've had plenty of time to dig herself a tunnel." He rubbed Clara's arm. "Can you find the spot where she had been digging?"

"I think so. It's on the far right, where the fence turns at a forty-five degree angle to come back to the house."

"Do you have a flashlight?"

Clara removed one from her kitchen junk drawer.

"Let's go. You lead the way."

Their progress was slow, but they followed the fence until they found the spot that Clara felt sure was where Noelle had been digging.

Kurt stooped and clawed at the two feet of snow now piled up against the fence. He'd dug a four-foot swath when he swung back to Clara and gave the thumbs-up sign. He'd uncovered a shallow trough, deep enough for a small dog to crawl through.

Clara dropped to her knees next to him, turning the flashlight on the spot. She looked into Kurt's eyes and nodded.

"We now know where to look." Kurt placed his lips close to Clara's ears. "Let's go back to the house and call the police."

He stood and pulled Clara to her feet. They made their way quickly back to the house, propelled by the certainty that a search and rescue operation was a necessity—and the sooner it got started, the better.

CHAPTER 18

Clara placed her hand over her phone and shook her head, mouthing the words "she hasn't heard from Ian."

Kurt raked his fingers through his hair.

"Don't try to come home, Laura," Clara said. "You'll never make it. It doesn't do Ian any good to have you stranded on the street."

"I can pick her up and bring her here," Kurt interjected. "I'll get through this."

"Did you hear that, Laura?" Clara said into the phone. She began nodding as she listened to Laura's response. "Tabitha's in a room for observation," she said to Kurt. "Laura insists she has to get out of there—to look for Ian."

Kurt picked up his keys and headed for the door.

"We're on our way, now. Wait by the entrance. We'll text when we get there." Clara swiped to end the call.

"You're not coming," Kurt said.

"*What?* It's my fault Ian's out there… in this…" her voice broke.

"You're not responsible." Kurt grasped her shoulders. "The police will be here any minute, and search and rescue soon after. You need to let them in and take them to the spot on the fence where we think Noelle got out."

Clara swallowed hard. Kurt was right. "Okay. Go. I'll text you Laura's number so you can call when you get there. Don't park to go inside. You might get stuck."

"I won't. Don't worry about me. It may take a while for us to get back here, but we'll make it."

"Do you think Ian went into that gully between the houses, looking for Noelle?"

"That's my best guess."

"They could freeze to death out there…"

"Stop it." Kurt gave her shoulders a quick shake. "We have no reason to think that. Ian's a mature, responsible young man. Even if he didn't go to a friend's house, he probably made it to one of the houses on either side of the gully. I'll bet he and Noelle are safe and warm, drinking hot chocolate in someone's kitchen."

"Then why hasn't he called his mother—or me—to tell us? He'd know how worried we'd be by now."

Kurt's lips pressed into a straight line. "There are a lot of explanations that don't end in disaster. Stay focused on what we know at the moment. Don't let your mind take you to horrible places."

"You're right," Clara said. "I'll be fine here. Go to Laura. She sounded like she was about to lose it."

They stepped into each other, sharing an embrace they both needed.

Clara was the first to step away.

"Call me when the police get here."

"Will do. Drive carefully, Kurt. Call me when you and Laura are on your way back."

Kurt stepped out the door and was swallowed by the storm.

Clara returned to the kitchen and paced. There had to be something she could do. Her eyes fell on a vibrant red knitted scarf that she'd deposited on the coat rack at the back door. She hadn't worn it since she'd received the luxurious cashmere one from Kurt.

Clara zipped her down jacket and snatched the red scarf from its hook. She had plans for it.

She wound her new scarf around her neck and tied it securely. Clara pulled her knit cap down around her ears, picked up the red scarf and flashlight, and headed into the backyard.

She felt her way along the side of the house until she found the fence. She struggled through the growing snow piled against the fence until she came to the place where the fence turned.

The snow that had fallen in the short time since she and Kurt had returned to the house almost obliterated the area where Noelle had dug under the fence. Clara bent over and dug at the base of the fence, as she'd seen Kurt do. Within minutes, she was satisfied she'd found the correct spot.

Clara pulled the red scarf from her pocket and forced one end through a chain link at the top of the fence. She wound it over on itself and tied it in a triple knot.

Clara sucked a deep breath of the icy air and trained her flashlight in front of her. The scarf cut a red slash against the endless white, marking the spot where Noelle and Ian had most likely entered the gully. She hoped this would help search and rescue. It wasn't much, but it was the only thing she could think to do to help.

Her flashlight beam flickered, and she shut it off. Clara didn't have extra batteries on hand, and she might need it later, if the power went out. She could safely retrace the path to the house by running one hand along the fence.

Clara was turning to retrace her steps when a spot in the snow, on the other side of the chain-link, began to glow. She blinked and looked again. There was definitely a light.

Clara wondered if her mind was playing tricks on her, but she swore she heard a cell phone ring. She bent and shoved her hand through the fence, lunging toward the illuminated spot in the snow.

Her hand found the small rectangular object. She gripped it with her gloved hand and pulled it back through the fence. The screen of the phone told her mom was calling.

Clara yanked her glove from her left hand while she clutched the phone with her right and stabbed at the screen. She brought it to her ear, the quavering voice on the other end of the line unmistakable.

"IAN," Laura choked on the word.

Clara's voice wavered. "It's me, Clara."

"What? Is he… is he with you?" came the tortured reply.

"No. I found his phone in my backyard."

Laura unleashed the sobs she'd been holding back.

Clara pressed Ian's phone to her ear and resumed her journey to her back door. "This is good information for the police," she said calmly. "It gives them a good idea where to start searching."

Laura continued to cry until she was interrupted by clicking sounds on her phone. "That's Kurt," Laura said. "He's here." She ended the call.

Clara pulled the phone away from her ear and secured it in her pocket. Alone in the dark night, with the wind howling around her, she prayed her confident assertion to Laura was justified.

CHAPTER 19

Ian kept his head lowered and his face to the ground as his legs pistoned up and down in the deep snow. His breathing came in labored gasps. Noelle nestled warm and snug against his chest, but she was becoming heavy. He pulled his scarf up to cover the tip of his nose, now numb with cold.

He planted his right foot firmly in front of him, but it didn't go down to the level of his left foot, throwing him off balance. He leaned back, throwing his arms out to steady himself.

For the first time since he'd found Noelle, he looked directly in front of himself. The swirling snow had a reddish cast. Ian peered into the night as the snow ebbed and flowed. There was a brick wall not ten feet in front of him.

Ian staggered forward, one arm outstretched, while the other supported Noelle. He was right. They'd found a building. The uneven terrain that had caused him to stumble must have been a curb or sidewalk.

Ian pressed his side against the wall as he followed its path. He soon found a metal door with a large, mullioned glass pane in the upper half. There was something familiar about this door. He pressed his face to the glass, but couldn't make out anything inside.

Ian pounded on the door. No one answered. He tried the heavy latch. The door was locked.

Ian continued to navigate along the wall, wracking his brain to remember where he'd seen that door.

The wall took a sharp left turn and brought him to a set of double glass doors. The push-bar type handle told him this was not a house.

Snow clung to the glass, and he rubbed it away with a gloved hand. He narrowed his eyes at the block letters painted on the door.

All Saints Church, Daycare, and Preschool. Administration.

His heart jumped to his throat, and he leaned his forehead against the glass and moaned. He knew this place. He'd spent weekdays here, the first five years of his life, while his mother taught chemistry at Pinewood High School. All Saints was less than a mile from his house. He felt like he'd been walking for hours—he didn't think he'd be this close to home.

The door with the half window led to the Sunday school classrooms. The sanctuary was across the parking lot behind him, and the preschool wing was to his right. Ian moved in that direction. He wondered if they'd ever repaired the lock on the window into the four-year-olds' classroom. He remembered when a raccoon had gotten in one weekend and made a colossal mess. The teachers had been beside themselves, but all the kids thought it was neat and pleaded that the creature be allowed to stay.

Bolstered by hope, Ian made his way to the four-year-olds' classroom window on the far side of the preschool wing of the building. If he couldn't open the window, he'd break it. He and Noelle couldn't survive out in the storm much longer.

Ian removed his gloves and reached for the metal sash that ran horizontally through the middle of the window. His flesh stuck to the freezing metal, and he quickly pulled his hands away. He'd need to do this with gloves on.

He tried again and again, but his gloved hands slipped off the metal. He pursed his lips. One more try and then he'd kick the window in.

Ian pressed the sides of his palms into the glass and slowly applied pressure to the sash. He was about to give up when he heard a pop and the window moved. With steady effort, Ian raised the lower pane of glass. The opening was just wide enough to allow him to push his torso through and tumble to the floor inside.

Noelle yelped when they hit the ground.

"Sorry, girl." Ian rolled and got to his feet. He unzipped his jacket and allowed Noelle to jump out.

Ian went to the window and slammed it shut against the snow and wind. He felt his way along the wall until he located a light switch. He flicked it on and off, but nothing happened. The chilly temperature in the room registered in his consciousness.

"The power's out," he said to Noelle. He reached out to the wall phone that had hung next to the light switch. Ian brought the receiver to his ear, but there was no dial tone.

He wouldn't be able to let his mother or Clara know where he was.

Noelle came to him and placed her front paws on his knee.

He knelt and patted her. "We've made it, Noelle. It may be cold, but we'll be fine until morning. I went to school here. They have pillows and blankets for nap time. And cots—too tiny for me now. And food," he said, suddenly aware that he was starving. "There'll be a snack cupboard. We'll at least have goldfish crackers and fruit snacks. All we have to do is find it. First—let's get you some water."

Ian began walking across the room, Noelle prancing at his heels. He yelped as his knee connected with a low table.

"I guess I'd better use my flashlight." Ian located the low sink where he'd lined up to wash hands at lunchtime when he'd been a student. He found a bowl on a shelf above the sink and filled it with water, setting it down in front of Noelle.

She lapped up a long drink while Ian lowered his mouth to the faucet and quenched his thirst.

He next located the snack cupboard and had soon consumed the next week's allotment of crackers, cookies, and other treats. By the time he'd built them a nest on the floor of layered blankets and pillows, he knew he'd sleep like a rock.

Ian loosened the laces on his boots but decided it was too cold in the room to remove them. He burrowed into the blankets and patted the spot next to him.

Noelle moved toward him, then stopped, her head turned over her shoulder and her ears perked.

"Come on, Noelle," Ian said around a yawn. "There's

nothing else for us to do tonight. We're going to have to wait it out until morning. May as well get some sleep."

Noelle wagged her tail in acknowledgment but remained at attention.

"Come on, Noelle," Ian repeated. "I'm..." he stopped abruptly and listened.

CHAPTER 20

"Of course you can," Josef spoke into his cell phone. Maisie hovered in the doorway to the kitchen, listening to his side of the conversation.

"Ten minutes? I'll watch for you." He tapped the screen to end the call.

"Who's coming here in this weather?" Maisie asked.

"That was the Highway Patrol. They need shelter for stranded motorists they've picked up on the highway. They've already got a dozen people and they have nowhere to take them."

"The diner won't be very comfortable for them. It'll be warm and safe, but there's nowhere to lie down," Maisie said. "Is the Pinewood Springs Motel available?"

Josef shook his head. "Motorists realized the highway would become impassable, and the motel was full by dinnertime. I thought we'd let the highway patrol use the bakery building. Now that it's cleaned out, they can bring in cots or sleeping bags."

"We don't own it anymore, remember?" She turned her

head to one side and arched an eyebrow. "The sale to the Pinewood Springs Motel closed yesterday."

"About that." Josef cleared his throat. "It didn't."

"What are you talking about?"

"The motel backed out of the deal. They couldn't get financing."

"Josef! When did you find out?"

He took a deep breath before answering. "Last week."

"Is that what you and Kurt were talking about in your office the night you got home so late?"

Josef nodded.

"Why didn't you tell me?"

"You've been so down in the dumps. Our broker said we'll have another offer soon. I figured I'd wait until then."

Maisie crossed her arms over her chest. "We've always told each other everything. Now's not the time to change that. I don't care that the sale fell through."

"Really?"

"I was never crazy about having a workout room there. Maybe now we'll have a neighbor in the space that will do something interesting." She crossed the kitchen to the back door and picked up her snow boots. She sat at the breakfast table to put them on.

"What're you doing? It's a blizzard out there."

"When the highway patrol officer arrives to pick up the key, you'll go with them." She lifted her eyes to his. "You'll want to open the diner and feed those poor people who've been rescued from their cars."

Josef pursed his lips and turned his head aside.

"You can't help yourself—you always want to help

people." She went to him and slipped her arms around his waist. "It's one of the things I admire most about you."

"The highway patrol will bring aid workers with them. I'll show them how to operate the grill and coffee machine, and the patrol will bring me back home."

"I'm going with you." She stood and threw her shoulders back. "We're going to open the diner and cook for these poor people, just like we did during that huge blizzard that hit right after we'd purchased the diner."

"That was forty years ago, sweetheart."

"I remember it vividly because it was one of the most rewarding things I've ever done. I'd like to feel that way again."

"It was a ton of hard work. I don't know if we have the stamina."

"You said they're bringing aid workers."

"Yes."

"So we won't be doing this alone. Even if we were, I've recovered my strength." She walked to him and put her hands on either side of his face. "What I'm still missing, after my stroke, is my sense of purpose. This won't be a permanent solution, but it's what I need right now."

"There's a sofa in my office," Josef said. "We can take turns sleeping there."

"That's a great idea. The storm is supposed to pass in the morning. It's just one night. We can do this."

Maisie went to the front door and removed her coat from the closet. She saw, through the window in the door, a set of headlights turn off the street and into their driveway.

"They're here," she called over her shoulder as she slipped her arms into her coat.

Josef joined her. "Do you have your medications, in case we're there for a while?"

Maisie hoisted her purse onto her shoulder. "They're in here."

Josef reached for the door handle and they looked at each other and grinned. "This is going to be fun," he said.

"Much better than sitting at the window, watching it snow!"

Josef opened the door, and they stepped over the threshold to greet the waiting patrol officer.

"You've never scrambled an egg?" Maisie's brows shot up as she looked at the young man poking at the rubbery pellets of egg that would have been soft curds if they'd been taken off the heat eight minutes earlier.

He shook his head. "I'm a new volunteer. Haven't finished my training. They were shorthanded, so they put me on this crew. The other guy doesn't know how to cook, either." He scraped at a wide swatch of burned-on egg along the side of the pan. "Do you think these are all right to eat? They sent us with supplies, but this was all the eggs, so I don't want to throw them out."

Maisie took the spatula from him and turned the mixture over. "We've got plenty of eggs in our cooler. Are there any pets in the group?"

"I saw a couple of big dogs."

"Let's save these for the pups and start over for the

people. I can teach you, if you'd like to learn." She tilted the overcooked eggs into a Styrofoam container.

"Is it hard to learn? I've only ever used the microwave."

"Easiest thing in the world," Maisie said. "Wash this pan while I get another couple dozen eggs."

The volunteer followed Maisie's directions. At first, he'd had to fish broken bits of shell out of the bowl every time he cracked an egg. By the time he'd completed the second dozen, the liquid egg slipped across the straight edge of the cracked shell and into the bowl without a trace of shell.

"Look at you!" Maisie praised. "You've got it."

"Once you know how hard to tap the shell on the rim of the bowl, it's easy." His smile reflected his sense of accomplishment.

Maisie handed him a whisk. "Break up the yolks and stir all that together with this."

He set to the task with vigor, sending a stream of egg over the side of the bowl. "That's too hard." He slowed his hand motion. "Like this?"

Maisie nodded. She put a large slab of butter into the pan and turned on the burner. "When the yolks and whites are thoroughly combined, pour half the mixture into the pan. We'll cook them in two batches."

He did as he was told.

Maisie showed how to stir the mixture, continually circling the sides of the pan and flipping over the cooked eggs on the bottom of the pan. She stepped aside. "Now you try it. The trick is to keep the eggs moving in the pan and take them off the heat the instant they set. It doesn't take long."

The volunteer finished the eggs, sliding the pan off the burner at precisely the right time. He turned to Maisie, a grin on his face. "They look good, don't they?"

Maisie chuckled and patted his arm. "Couldn't be better. They'll be delicious."

"I'll put these under our warming lights," Maisie said. "Can you cook the other eggs you've prepared without my help?"

"I've got this."

"Good. I'll see if Josef found any fruit we can contribute."

"We brought sleeves of those little white donuts with us."

"Everyone loves those. The coffee is done brewing, too."

"We've also got school lunch-size milk cartons."

Maisie looked at the big clock over the rear door. "Two in the morning is an odd time to serve breakfast."

"Everyone was hungry, and no one was sleeping, so that's why the other volunteer and I decided we should make them something to eat."

"Do either of you have a food handler's license?"

"I don't," he said, his eyes growing big. "Do I need one?"

"Don't worry. I've got you covered."

He finished the eggs as Josef emerged from the cooler with one bag containing oranges and another full of bananas.

"We'll combine the eggs into this foil pan," Josef said. "I'll fill a couple of insulated dispensers with coffee while you take the eggs and fruit to the bakery building."

The volunteer retrieved his jacket from a chair in the corner and suited up to go into the storm. "I'll come back for the coffee," he said. "I can take the eggs and fruit in one trip."

Maisie loaded him up.

The young man moved to the door, then turned back to Maisie. "Thanks for showing me how to scramble eggs," he said. "You're a great teacher. This was really fun."

Maisie's smile stretched from ear to ear. "It was fun for me, too. You're a natural. I hope you keep learning."

"If I could take lessons from you, I definitely would." He opened the door and stepped into the swirling snow.

Maisie shut the door quickly against the wind and leaned her back against it. She was an excellent teacher. And she loved it. The best times she'd had recently had been teaching Kurt to make a Valentine's Day dinner, and now this.

Maisie went to the window overlooking the back parking lot and the former bakery. The light above the building was barely visible through the snow. A thought whispered gently in her mind. Maybe she'd hit on the perfect new use for the building.

Josef interrupted her reverie as he brought the coffee dispensers to the counter next to the door as it flew open. The volunteer crossed the threshold, buoyed by the wind.

"They finished all those eggs before I finished laying out the fruit," he said.

"Then let's make more," Maisie said, winking at Josef.

Josef fetched another two dozen eggs from the cooler and the volunteer got busy, as if he'd been scrambling eggs for decades.

Maisie stood back and watched. Josef came up beside

her and slipped his arm around her shoulders. "You're right. Coming here tonight has restored you."

Maisie turned to him. "You have no idea." She drew a deep breath. "I think I know what I want to do with myself."

"Oh?"

"And it means keeping the bakery building. Can we afford to do that?"

"Sure. What're you thinking?"

"I'm not ready to say just yet. I'd like to do some research and think my idea through."

"That's fine."

"Once I've worked out the details, I'll talk to you."

"What can I do to help?"

"Would you tell our broker we're taking the building off the market?" Maisie flashed the smile at him that still made his heart flip-flop.

Josef held her close. "I'll do that first thing in the morning."

CHAPTER 21

Noelle raced from their makeshift bed on the floor to the door of the classroom and back again. She leapt toward Ian, her front paws resting on his chest. Her tail wagged with urgency.

"What's gotten into you?"

Noelle emitted two quick barks and sprinted to the door.

Ian pushed himself to a sitting position. His shoulders sagged. Now that he was safely indoors, the adrenaline rush that had propelled him earlier had dissipated. He was bone tired. Ian turned his back to Noelle and laid down again, resting his head on his arm.

Noelle pawed at the interior door and barked furiously.

"You're not giving up, are you?" Ian muttered as he forced himself onto his feet. He walked to the door and opened it. "Show me," he said, covering a yawn with his hand.

Noelle bounded down the corridor and came to a stop at a windowless door tucked under the stairs.

Ian switched on his flashlight and trained it on the door. It was either a broom closet or small storage room.

Noelle swiped at the door and paused.

They both listened. A faint meowing emanated from behind the door.

Noelle looked back at Ian and uttered a soft woof.

"I heard it, girl." Ian bent over and pulled Noelle back. "There's a cat—or cats—in there. They may not be as eager to meet you as you are to say hello to them." He positioned her six feet behind him. "Sit," he commanded, then "stay."

Noelle obeyed and brushed her tail along the floor, panting in anticipation.

Ian turned the handle and opened the door slowly. He shined the fading light of the flashlight inside.

Three pairs of eyes stared back at him, blinking in the sudden brightness.

"Kittens," Ian said, looking over his shoulder to address Noelle. He shone his light around the interior of the small broom closet.

"We've got three kittens. There's no sign of a mother cat."

The kittens were nestled in a pile of rags on the floor. They squirmed against each other and continued to meow, but didn't try to escape.

Ian dropped to his knees and reached out a hand to the litter, allowing them to smell him. "You're young. I'll bet you can't walk yet, can you?"

One kitten touched Ian's hand with its nose while the others turned away.

Ian extended his fingers and stroked the side of the kitten's face. "It's colder here than in the classroom," he said. He sat back on his heels. "We need to take you with us. I haven't got anything for you to eat or drink—except water—but we can get you to the vet tomorrow. If the storm stops," he added, under his breath.

He removed his jacket and spread it out at his feet. Ian scooped up the kittens, one by one, and placed them onto his jacket. They squirmed their way to the spot that was still warm from his body.

The kittens continued to meow, but none of them struggled or protested.

Noelle, who had been leaning forward as far as she could without toppling over, uttered a woof that could only be described as a doggie whisper.

Ian looked into the dog's pleading eyes.

"Okay, girl. You're the one who found them. You have to be gentle, but come say hello."

Noelle eased her way forward, gingerly sniffing at the squirming bundle of kittens.

One kitten turned to Noelle and hissed.

Noelle jumped back.

"It's all right, Noelle. They're tiny, and they've probably never met a dog before. They're scared of you." Ian stood and gathered up his coat with its content of kittens.

They walked back to the classroom.

Ian took a blanket from the bed he had fashioned on the floor for himself and made a nest for the kittens. He positioned it on the floor next to his bed and moved the kittens to their new home.

"I know you need mother's milk," he said, "but I don't have any. If you're thirsty, the best I can do is water." He went to the sink, filled a shallow bowl with water, and brought it to the kittens.

Lifting them one by one, he held them over the bowl so they could lap up a drink.

The friendly kitten from earlier sniffed at the water but didn't drink. The others were indifferent as well. Ian wet his fingers and held them out to the kittens. None of them licked him.

Noelle watched from a cautious distance.

"That's the best I can do." Ian sighed in resignation and yawned again. "We all need sleep." He put his jacket on again and zipped it shut against the increasing cold in the room.

He bundled himself into the blankets on the floor and turned onto his side. Noelle curled herself into a ball and nestled against his chest.

Ian didn't know how long he had been asleep when a commotion at the window woke him.

Noelle had jumped onto a table that was pushed against the wall under the window. Her front paws rested on the glass. She peered out the window as she sidestepped along the table. Her tail wagged furiously.

"Noelle!" Ian didn't hide his irritation. "Get away from there. I'm trying to sleep."

Noelle looked back at him and uttered a sharp bark, then returned her attention to the window.

"This is just like before," Ian grumbled. He began to turn over, then halted abruptly. "Just like before," he said as he became fully awake.

He leapt to his feet and joined Noelle at the window.

"What's out there, girl? What do you see?"

NOELLE'S front paws whirred against the window. Moonlight pierced the gaps in the clouds, creating an eerie brightness in the snow.

"You can't dig yourself out of here, girl," Ian said. He cupped his hands around his face and pressed them to the window. "The snow's still coming down fast, but the wind isn't blowing so hard. Maybe the storm's moving away from Pinewood." He focused on the courtyard outside the window. "I don't see what's got you all worked up."

Noelle barked in response and kept clawing at the glass.

Ian pursed his lips. Noelle had been right about the kittens. What if someone was trapped out there? They would never survive until morning, even if the storm was abating.

He retrieved his knit cap and Noelle's leash from the floor by his bed. "We're not going far," he said. "I won't lose sight of this building."

Noelle hopped off the table and landed at his feet, wagging her tail so hard she almost fell over.

"Stop squirming," Ian said as he grasped her collar and clipped the leash to it. He squatted next to her and took her face in his hands. "Show me what's out there, girl."

They went to the door at the end of the room that opened onto the courtyard. It swung outward. He pushed the attached metal doorstop into the downward position and shoved it into the snow. He tested it to make sure the door wouldn't slam shut and lock behind them.

"We're letting even more cold air into the room, so we have to be quick," he said.

Noelle strained against the leash.

Ian didn't correct her, but allowed her to lead the way.

Noelle floundered in the deep snow but pressed forward, intent on her destination. She kept going, with Ian tromping along behind her.

A high hedge of an evergreen shrub was in front of them. Noelle tugged harder.

They reached the hedge and Noelle burrowed into the base, flinging snow behind her with her front paws.

A high-pitched screech that sounded like a scream soon interrupted the quiet night, followed by hissing.

Noelle yipped and backed out of the hedge fast, swiping her paw over her nose.

Ian stooped to examine her. "You got whacked on the nose, didn't you?"

Noelle continued to back away.

"I think you've found the mama cat." Ian slowly parted the branches of the shrub and peered into the dark interior. "Hello, there. We won't hurt you."

He waited and watched. A slight movement caught his eye. "Your kittens are safe inside," he said in soothing tones. "Were you out here foraging for food?"

A pink nose set in a gray and white face emerged from the interior of the shrub.

"That's a good girl," Ian cooed. "Why don't you come inside with us? I think your kittens are hungry." He paused again. If she was a feral cat, he'd never persuade her to come with him.

The cat extended one front paw toward him and took a tentative step forward.

Ian held his breath. He wished he had a treat to offer her.

She took another step.

Noelle leaned around Ian to investigate.

The cat retreated quickly.

"Noelle," Ian said firmly. "You're not helping. Sit and stay."

Noelle gave Ian a reproachful look, but obeyed.

"Come on," Ian said. "It's cold out here."

The cat advanced again.

Ian rested his right palm face-up in the snow.

The cat sniffed it, then rolled onto her side and rubbed the top of her head against his hand.

Ian brought his left hand to her side and stroked her.

The gray and white tabby purred.

Ian smiled and cautiously gathered her up, brushing snow from her coat.

The cat didn't protest.

Ian held her against his chest and lumbered to his feet.

Noelle watched with rapt attention but didn't insert herself into the scene. Once more, she led the way.

The party of three made their way to the classroom.

Ian kicked the snow out of the doorway that had fallen in the short time he and Noelle had been gone. He slammed the door shut.

A faint mewing came from the nest of kittens.

The tabby leapt from Ian's arms and raced across the room to them. She inserted herself in their midst, kneading the blanket with her paws. A chorus of high-pitched trills signaled their delight at having their mother back.

"You were right again, Noelle. That's the mother cat, for sure. Now those kittens will have what they need." He sat on the floor and drew Noelle into his lap. "You've been very brave tonight. You should get an award for saving lives."

Noelle yawned as he gave her a good rub.

"I think we're both ready to drop," he said. He placed her on the floor and stood. "Let's crawl into our bed." He moved toward the blankets spread out on the floor.

Noelle remained where she was.

"Come on, Noelle."

She didn't budge.

"Are you afraid of that mama cat?"

Noelle stared up at him.

"Who could blame you? I wouldn't want to sleep next to someone who'd whacked my nose with razor-sharp claws."

Ian dragged their make-shift bed away from the kittens and their mother, over to where Noelle sat, rooted to the floor. He lowered himself into place, and Noelle stretched out against him.

The last thing Ian heard before he fell asleep was Noelle's rumbling snores.

CHAPTER 22

Kurt turned the corner onto Laura's street. Flashing red and blue lights were dimly visible through the heavy blanket of falling snow.

"Those are police cars—and they're at my house. There's a bunch of them." Laura turned to Kurt. "Do you think they found him?"

"We'll know soon enough."

A strangled cry escaped her lips. "You don't think they found his…" her voice trailed off.

"Absolutely not. Don't think that. It's probably the search and rescue teams."

"Clara promised to call us when they arrived." Laura's voice was shrill.

Kurt's phone vibrated with the incoming call. He pressed a button on his steering wheel and answered it.

"Search and rescue just arrived. They've got a team of ten," Clara said.

"That's great. I was worried that more of them would be busy rescuing stranded motorists."

"A boy on foot is more urgent," Clara said.

Laura moaned and lowered her face to her hands.

"They need to talk to me," Clara said as she disconnected the call.

"We're four houses away." Kurt glanced at Laura. "I don't think we can get any closer without blocking police access. I'm going to pull over here. Can you walk the rest of the way?"

Laura brought her head up sharply. "I'll walk through walls of fire to get to Ian."

Kurt slid into a snowdrift at the curb.

Laura was out of the car and floundering toward her house before Kurt could get his seat belt unfastened.

He caught up with Laura and grabbed her elbow, putting his mouth close to her ear. "Let's move to the middle of the street and walk in the tracks made by the police vehicles. It'll be easier."

Laura followed Kurt.

Two police cars and five search and rescue vehicles blocked the street, their flashing lights slicing ribbons of color across the snow.

Kurt took Laura's arm again and helped her climb the steep driveway to the main house.

A uniformed officer stood at the rear door. He waved them in the direction of the guest house. "They're all down there."

Laura pushed herself to move faster, slipping and sliding as she went.

The guest house door stood open. Officers and workers with green reflective vests moved in and out.

Laura stepped into the chaos, with Kurt right behind her.

Clara entered the hallway from the kitchen and saw them standing in the entryway. She wove her way through the hustle and bustle of people talking on headsets and consulting maps.

"You're just in time," she said. "The search and rescue teams are about to set out. The organizer is over there." Clara pointed to a stocky man with salt and pepper hair and a take-charge demeanor. "Do you want to talk to him before we leave?" She put an arm around Laura's shoulders.

"I'm not staying here!" Laura pulled away from Clara. "I need to be out there, looking for him."

"Someone should wait at your house, in case he calls or comes home," Kurt said.

Laura's eyes shot daggers at him. "We'll leave it unlocked." She emphasized each word. "I'll put a note and his phone on the kitchen table, telling him I'm out with search and rescue and to call me and 911 when he gets home." She swung to Clara.

"That should do it," Clara said. "I would insist on going out there to search for him, too. In fact," her face flushed, "I already did. They wanted both of us to stay behind. I've already taped a similar note to my refrigerator."

A smile flitted across Laura's lips. "He'll definitely find it there. He must be starved..." Her voice cracked.

"I'll tell them that the three of us will work as a team," Kurt said. "They're assigning search tasks now." He walked up to the man in charge.

Clara and Laura watched as the man shook his head "no." Kurt continued talking until the man shrugged and finally nodded in agreement. The man made notations on a map on his clipboard and showed it to Kurt. They huddled together as the search-and-rescue leader talked and Kurt listened.

Kurt finally rejoined Clara and Laura. "Two teams have already set out along the gully between your street and the one behind you."

"That's where we think Noelle got out of my yard," Clara said, her voice wavering. "And Ian went after her."

"Three teams will begin going door-to-door on this street and the ones around it. They feel the most likely outcome is that Ian took shelter in one of the houses and no one has called because the power is out."

"Cell phones still work," Laura said, her tone full of despair.

"It's the end of the day and people's batteries may be dead. Since the power's out, they can't recharge them."

"You can recharge a cell phone from a laptop," Laura said, her voice a monotone.

"We don't know what's happened and we're wasting time speculating," Kurt said, bringing the discussion to a close. "The leader has assigned us the houses from the beginning of this street to the end."

"That must be over a dozen houses," Laura said.

"Are you ready?"

Laura nodded in the affirmative.

"Let's get going," Kurt said.

Clara tied her scarf under her chin and tucked her hair into her cap.

They set out in single file, following Laura.

CLARA WALKED Noelle up and down this street every day. The usually easy trek was treacherous in the snow that now reached to her knees. Five-foot drifts concealed walkways and obstructed doorways. They couldn't tell where the sidewalk began, and the street ended. On four of the last five houses, they'd had to circle the house until they'd found a window they could rap on to get the owner's attention. They plodded their way to the next house, relieved that the front door was unobstructed by snow.

"A widower lives here," Laura said, as they stepped onto the porch. "I've known Mr. Barnes my whole life."

Kurt raised his fist and knocked firmly on the door.

The three of them waited, turning their backs to the wind and stomping their feet to keep warm.

No one answered.

Kurt knocked again.

There was no reply.

"Maybe he's not home," Clara said.

Laura shook her head. "He's virtually homebound and has no family. He's got to be in there."

"Maybe he's sound asleep and doesn't hear us," Kurt said. He pounded on the door.

The door remained firmly shut, the windows dark behind closed curtains.

"I don't have a good feeling about this," Laura said. "Could we call in a welfare check?"

"Sure. The police are probably getting a lot of those calls tonight."

Laura pursed her lips. "They wouldn't get here right

away. And—forgive me for saying this—I don't want to pull anyone away from looking for Ian."

"We can't break in," Kurt said.

Clara snapped her fingers. "What if he's hidden a key out here somewhere?"

"That's a great idea," Laura said. "We'll do our own welfare check."

They began running their hands over the top of the door and the adjacent windows. Clara examined a large pot next to the door that, come spring, would hold flowers.

Laura felt around the light fixture by the door. "Found it!" she called in triumph as she pulled a small magnetic box from the top of the fixture. She shook the box and the rattling noise confirmed it contained a key.

Laura opened the box and dumped the key into her hand. "I'll go inside first," she said. "Mr. Barnes knows me, so it'll be less scary for him."

The key fit the lock and the door opened noiselessly. "Mr. Barnes. It's Laura Ramsey—your neighbor."

They stepped inside, and Laura called to him again, this time raising her voice.

They were picking their way cautiously across the living room when Clara halted and put up a hand in a 'stop' gesture.

Everyone stopped and listened.

A soft moan came from the top of the stairs.

Kurt turned to the stairs they'd passed on their way in, and took them two at a time.

Clara and Laura were right behind him.

A tiny, frail man lay on his stomach at the top of the stairs.

Kurt stepped to one side and placed the emergency call.

Laura dropped to her knees on the top step and put her hand lightly on his back. "Mr. Barnes. It's Laura from down the street."

He stirred and tried to rise.

"Stay where you are. We're calling for help."

He moaned again.

"Can you hear us, Mr. Barnes?" Clara asked.

He nodded slightly.

"Are you having a heart attack? Is there aspirin or medication we can give you?"

"No," he grunted in response.

Laura put her hand over his on the carpet.

"Paramedics are on their way, sir," Kurt said. He put his phone into flashlight mode and illuminated the scene.

The man's left leg jutted out at an odd angle. A cat sprinted away from the light, into a bedroom.

"Your leg looks like it's broken," Kurt said.

"Did you fall?" Laura asked.

Mr. Barnes forced out the words with some effort. "Tripped over that damned cat."

"I'm so sorry," Laura said.

"Good… you're… here," he said. "God… knows… how… long—"

"Don't you worry about a thing," Laura said. "Help's on the way and we'll be with you until it gets here." Her voice was firm, but her shoulders sagged.

"I'll stay with Mr. Barnes," Clara said. "The two of you should keep looking."

"Are you sure?" Laura asked.

"Of course I am. I won't leave his side. Who knows how long it'll take for the paramedics to get here."

"That's a great idea," Kurt said.

"When they're done here, I'll make my way back to the house and wait for you there."

"Thank you, Clara," Laura said. "You're going to be fine, Mr. Barnes. You're in good hands with Clara."

He nodded but didn't speak.

Laura hurried down the stairs.

"I don't like the idea of you walking back to the house alone," Kurt said quietly to Clara.

"Don't worry about me. It may be my imagination, but I think the storm's abating. If there are whiteout conditions when I'm leaving, I'll stay put here instead. I'm sure the paramedics won't throw me out into the storm."

"If they try, you call me." He kissed the tip of her nose and followed Laura out the door.

CHAPTER 23

Ian opened one eye a crack. He lay in the same position he'd fallen asleep in. The spot where Noelle had curled against him was empty. He glanced toward the cat and her kittens. All was peaceful in that direction.

Noelle scratched at the door and whimpered.

Ian pushed himself onto an elbow. "Do you need to go out?"

Noelle emitted a high-pitched whine.

Ian got to his feet and shuffled to the door.

Noelle shot out into the courtyard the moment he opened it.

Ian took a half step forward, straddling the threshold. He glanced at the sky. Snow continued to fall at a gentle pace and the winds had died down. A wide swath of light appeared on the horizon.

Noelle finished her business and raced back to the door, squeezing past Ian into the classroom.

Ian's stomach rumbled as he shut the door behind them.

Noelle took a drink from the bowl he'd placed on the floor for her. When she was done, she sat at his feet and brushed her tail along the floor.

"You want your breakfast, don't you? Me too. Except we have nothing to eat." He turned to the window. It was definitely getting lighter outside.

Ian flipped the light switch, but nothing happened. He picked up the phone. There was still no dial tone.

"We're not far from home, girl," he said to Noelle. "Less than a mile. I know the way. It's still snowing, but it's not like last night. Do you think you can walk?"

Noelle jumped against his leg and wagged her tail.

"It'll be fully daylight soon. I've got a few things to do before we leave here."

Ian made his way to the teacher's desk along the opposite wall and sat in the chair. He found a piece of paper and pen in a drawer and wrote his note.

Sorry about eating all your snacks and any mess I made. My dog and I were lost in the storm and we broke in so we could survive. My mom will pay for everything and I can come by after school to clean up.

Thank you,

Ian Ramsey and Noelle

PS—I went to preschool here.

Ian placed the note on the desktop and anchored it in place with a stapler. He folded the blankets he'd used for their bed and returned them and the pillows to the cupboard where he'd found them.

"You've got one last chance for a drink," he told Noelle, calling her to the bowl. She took another drink.

Ian put his mouth to the stream of water from the faucet and drank. He then picked up Noelle's bowl, washed it, and placed it in the cupboard.

"Now, for the kittens and that cat. We definitely need to take them with us."

Noelle uttered a short woof.

"I'm glad you agree." Ian found a cardboard box containing construction paper in the supply cabinet. He stacked the paper neatly on the teacher's desk and went to the kittens.

The mama cat lay on her side, the kittens nestled on the blanket against her.

Ian dragged the blanket out from under them. "Sorry about this," he said.

The cat and kittens stirred and howled in protest.

Ian lined the box with the blanket. "I'm going to take you with me," he told them. "My mother loves cats. Our cat died last fall. She's been talking about getting a new one. You'll get food at our house and maybe we'll keep you."

He picked up a gray kitten with one white paw and a black zigzag on its forehead that squirmed almost out of reach. He placed it on the blanket in the box. The kitten rose on unsteady haunches and clawed at the air.

The mama cat sat up and stretched, watching Ian closely.

The next kitten wriggled in his hand, its ginger-colored fur so silky and fine that he almost lost his grip on it.

The mama cat batted at his hand; her claws extended.

Ian yelped in pain but didn't drop the kitten, placing it into the box with its litter mates.

The mother cat jumped into the box in one fluid motion.

The third and final kitten remaining on the floor yowled. Ian extended his hand to it slowly. The black, blue-eyed kitten didn't protest. He placed it into the box. Ian watched the resulting sea of furry activity as they jostled and squirmed until they'd settled into position again.

Ian returned to the desk and penned a second post-script to his note.

I took a blanket with me for the cat and kittens. I'll bring it back.

"I think that's all we can do, Noelle." He looked at the window. "It's light out, now."

He zipped his coat and put on his cap and gloves, then picked up the box of felines. Ian covered them with part of the blanket to protect them from the cold and walked to the door. "I don't think you can run very fast or far in this snow, Noelle, but you need to stay with me. I don't want to chase you. Understand?" He looked down at her.

Noelle turned serious brown eyes on him and swished her tail slowly.

Ian opened the door and stepped outside, Noelle at his heels. "It's time to go home."

CHAPTER 24

The paramedics secured the straps on the gurney, making sure that the elderly man with the broken leg—and probably hip—was snugly wrapped in his blanket.

"Time to go for a ride, Mr. Barnes," one paramedic said. "We're going to take you down these stairs and out to our ambulance. Your friend has been shoveling a path for us. We've got a blizzard out there, but we'll get you safely to the hospital." The two men cautiously descended the stairs and brought the gurney out the front door.

Clara had almost reached the ambulance when she heard the rattle of the gurney as it crossed onto the porch. She didn't know how long she'd been shoveling. Her back ached and her fingers and toes were numb with cold.

She kicked her efforts into overdrive, determined to finish her task. She dug her shovel into the snow and threw it in a wide arc to the side. The muscles in her arms felt like they would burst into flame. Clara made one last pass as the gurney caught up with her.

"Thank you," a paramedic said. "This makes it much easier."

Clara stepped aside, leaning on her shovel, as she watched them load Mr. Barnes into the ambulance.

One paramedic slid behind the wheel while the other hopped in the rear next to their patient.

"Good luck, Mr. Barnes," Clara called.

The paramedic reached for the rear door. "Don't worry. We'll take good care of him."

Clara moved to the path she'd just cleared and watched the ambulance back down the driveway to the street and turn in the direction of the hospital. She checked her watch and was shocked to see that it was after seven in the morning. The paramedics had spent a long time assessing and attending to Mr. Barnes. She looked toward the horizon. It would be daylight soon.

She hurried into the garage and returned the shovel to its hook, then made a quick pass inside the house, turning off lights and making sure nothing had been left on the stove. Satisfied that his house would be fine until Mr. Barnes returned, Clara locked the front door and doggedly forced a trail through the fresh snow toward her house.

THE SNOWPLOW LUMBERED down the street, clearing a path. He'd encountered no one on the roads since he'd started his shift. The only obstacles he'd had to navigate around had been parked cars.

The driver nodded in satisfaction. It was barely snowing and was predicted to stop altogether by mid-morning. He and the other members of his crew would open up the city by late afternoon.

He glanced out his side window and surveyed the scene to his left. A lone figure in the distance trudged through the snow. He stared at the unlikely pedestrian walking at this early hour. His head snapped back when he realized a small dog pranced along next to the pedestrian.

It had to be.

He snatched his two-way radio from his dashboard and pushed the button. They'd been briefed about a missing sixth grader and a dog before they'd left the garage. "I think I've found that kid—and his dog," he said into the micro-phone, giving the location of the cross-streets where he'd seen Ian and Noelle. "They're plodding through the snow. I can't turn my truck. Want me to get out and go after them?"

The radio crackled. "Sending to police dispatch now. They'll find them. Continue on your route."

"Roger that," the driver said as he replaced the radio on the dash and watched the figures recede.

CHAPTER 25

Clara plodded through the deep snow up the driveway. There were no police vehicles at the curb; no flashing red and blue lights slicing through the early morning darkness. The lightly falling snow gave the scene a tranquil air that belied the desperate reality. Ian—and Noelle—were still missing.

Lights were on in the big house, but they'd left them on in case Ian came home. Clara climbed the steps to the back porch and opened the unlocked door, stepping inside. "Hello," she called, walking through the kitchen to the hallway. "Anyone here?"

Silence answered her question.

She exited the house and headed toward the guest cottage that she called home. She needed a bathroom break and a pair of dry gloves. A cup of coffee and a power bar would be helpful too. Clara knew she was running on adrenaline—and that she wouldn't stop until they found the boy and her dog.

She opened her front door, hoping against hope to find

Ian and Noelle asleep on the sofa. Her place was empty, the note she'd left for Ian untouched.

Clara went into the bathroom, leaning over the sink as she washed her hands and splashed water onto her face. She filled a cup with cold water and drank it down before pulling off her cap. Her hair was plastered to her skull. She gazed at her reflection in the mirror. She looked a fright, but right now she couldn't care less.

Clara toed off her boots and changed her socks before digging out a dry pair of gloves. She was headed for the kitchen to brew a cup of coffee when her cell phone buzzed with a call from Kurt.

"Where are you?" he asked before she could say anything. His words were choppy, as if he were working out.

"My house. What's happened?" Her stomach dropped to her knees, and she grabbed the kitchen doorframe for support.

"They've found them."

Clara shrieked and sank against the wall.

"A snowplow driver spotted them and called it in. They're on foot. We think they're headed for home. The police are on their way to where the driver saw him." He was panting with exertion.

"Thank God."

"We were nearly finished canvassing the street when Laura got the call from the police. We're almost back to my SUV. Laura wants to intercept them if we can. If you want to come, meet us at the curb."

Clara was already zipping up her jacket. "I'm on my way." She ran into the bedroom and snatched her cap and gloves. She headed out to Kurt's SUV, trudging through the snow as fast as she could go. She had to be part of this reunion.

Kurt and Laura were clawing at the snow imprisoning his SUV as Clara reached the top of the driveway. She raced to her car, which she'd thankfully left unlocked, and pulled the shovel from the trunk.

Kurt saw her coming toward them and held out his hands for the shovel. "You're a lifesaver," he said, taking it from her and quickly finishing the job. He pressed the unlock button on his key fob and Laura jumped into the front passenger seat while Clara climbed in behind her.

Kurt started his engine. His wheels spun, and he cursed under his breath. He flung his door open and raced to the back of his SUV, pulling out the bag of sand he kept on hand during the winter months. He ripped a hole in the plastic and poured sand in front of the back tires.

He flung himself behind the wheel again. Kurt put the SUV into reverse, then quickly switched into forward. The tires got traction, and he pulled away from the curb.

All three released the collective breath they'd been holding.

The snowfall had slowed to a dusting as the rising sun broke through the clouds. The pristine flakes falling in front of them sparkled like a sea of diamonds.

The vehicle crawled along through the foot of undisturbed snow on the street toward the location—less than a mile from the house—where Ian had been seen.

~

THE SUV INCHED up the incline of the unplowed street. They had just crested the hill when Kurt pumped the brakes. The SUV slid to a stop before driving into the wall of snow blocking the main street, deposited by the plow.

Kurt slapped the steering wheel with his fist. "I was afraid of this. They'll clear this out when they make a second pass to open the residential streets."

With a strangled moan, Laura bent over and placed her head in her hands.

Clara scooted to the edge of her seat, leaning over the center console to look out the windshield.

Kurt reached out to Laura. "I'm sorry. The police will find—"

"There!" Clara thrust her arm between them and pointed to the left side of the windshield. "It's them!"

Laura brought her face up and followed where Clara was pointing.

The familiar figures of a tall, lanky boy and a small brown and white dog were visible in the distance. The boy was carrying a cardboard box and walked slowly, matching the dog's plodding pace.

Laura flung her door open and hurtled herself into the snow. She held onto the car as she forced her way around it, her feet sinking into knee-deep snow.

Clara and Kurt were right behind her.

Laura clawed her way on hands and knees to the top of the wall of snow deposited by the plow. She stood, teetering unsteadily. "IAN," she screamed.

Kurt joined her in two strides. He cupped his mouth with his hands and called to the boy while Laura waved her hands over her head in wide arcs.

Clara reached the top in time to see Noelle pause and look at them. Noelle looked up at Ian and barked furiously. He looked down at the dog. Her tail pumped like a piston.

Kurt and Laura both called to Ian again.

Noelle swung her face in their direction and Ian looked up. He placed the cardboard box at his feet and raised his arms high over his head, sweeping his hands back and forth.

Laura slid down the other side of the wall of snow, landing on her bottom. She pushed herself to her feet and took off toward her son, her forward progress swift despite the snow.

Ian abandoned the kittens and struggled through the snow toward his mother.

Kurt jumped off the wall and turned back to Clara, holding out his hand to help her. They were soon following Laura.

A police siren sounded in the distance.

Laura and Ian fell into each other's arms. She swayed, and he steadied her.

"Ian." Laura gripped him tightly. "You're… I was so scared…" She let loose the tears she'd been holding back.

"I'm fine, Mom. I'm sorry I worried you—and that I couldn't call to tell you where I was." His voice trembled.

Laura sobbed.

"I shouldn't have gone after Noelle." Tears coursed down his cheeks. "We got lost. It was really scary. I thought… I didn't know…"

Laura kissed his cheek, swiping at the moisture left by their combined tears.

Kurt and Clara exchanged a glance as they caught up to

Laura and Ian. He motioned with his head toward Noelle. Clara nodded her agreement. They walked past the happy mother/son reunion and headed toward Clara's beloved pup.

Noelle yipped at them and wagged her tail, but she wouldn't leave the cardboard box.

Kurt reached them a half step ahead of Clara. He went directly for the box.

Clara held out her arms and Noelle leapt into them, snow flying like flour in her wake. Clara caught her and they fell to the ground. Noelle twisted and squirmed, covering her owner with fervent doggie kisses. Clara chortled and lay back in the snow, letting the irrepressible Noelle have her way with her.

Kurt smiled down at the woman he loved and her overjoyed dog.

Clara finally sat up. "That's enough now, Noelle."

The dog continued her ebullient greeting.

Clara stood and scooped Noelle into her arms, holding her securely against her chest. "Calm down, Noelle. Everything's okay."

Noelle licked Clara's neck one last time before turning her attention to Kurt.

A chorus of feline screeching emanated from the box.

Clara's eyes widened. "You've got a box of cats."

"One cat and three very tiny kittens, to be exact," Kurt said.

Noelle strained her muzzle toward the box.

"Ian found Noelle, and he rescued a cat and kittens, too?" Clara asked the rhetorical question.

"It appears so," Kurt said.

Noelle uttered a soft "woof."

Clara planted a kiss on the top of Noelle's head. "Are you telling us you helped save these felines?"

Noelle thumped her tail against Clara's side.

"I can't wait to hear the whole story," Kurt said.

Clara nodded. "I'll tell you what—that's one resourceful young man."

"I couldn't agree more."

"He deserves some sort of award or recognition."

"I was thinking the same thing." He looked at Clara and winked. "Let's make that happen."

Two police cars, sirens and lights engaged, pulled to a stop along the plowed street close to where Ian and Laura still clung to each other.

"Ian will soon be telling the police everything."

"Let's get over there. I don't want to miss a thing."

Burdened with a box of cats and a small dog, Kurt and Clara rejoined Laura and Ian as the police made their way to them.

CHAPTER 26

Kurt maneuvered his SUV into the spot at the curb he'd vacated little more than an hour earlier. Feeling the fatigue and tension of the past day catching up with her, Laura slowly got out as Ian went to the back of the SUV and removed the box of cats.

With Noelle in Clara's arms and the feline-filled box in Ian's, they all headed to the main house.

"I'm going to call the hospital to check on my grandmother," Laura said. "If she's doing all right, I'll slip into bed for a few hours of sleep."

"I'm starved," Ian said.

Laura covered a yawn with her hand. "I'll make you breakfast after I call the hospital."

Ian shook his head. "You're beat. I didn't sleep much either. I'm gonna eat a bowl of cereal and head to my room." He shifted the box in his hands. "Will these guys be okay? Should we take them to the vet?"

They wearily climbed the steps and walked into the kitchen, followed by Kurt, Clara, and Noelle.

Laura pulled back the blanket and peered into the box. Her gaze was met by four sets of bright eyes. The previously quiet cat and kittens now emitted a series of high-pitched meeps and meows.

Noelle pressed herself deeper into Clara's arms.

"Gosh—they're so small." Laura reached into the box and picked up a fuzzy orange ball of fluff, bringing it to her neck and nuzzling it.

The mother cat yowled in protest.

Laura planted a kiss on the top of the kitten's head and returned it to its mother.

Ian watched his mom, wide-eyed. "You're not mad that I brought them all home?"

"Of course not," Laura said, running a finger gently along the mother cat's back. "You couldn't leave them." She looked up at Ian. "If you hadn't rescued their mother from the storm, they all would have died."

"Maybe we can keep…" his voice trailed off.

"We'll see," Laura said, studying the kittens. "We were going to get a new cat soon, anyway."

Ian grinned. He knew his mother was a pushover. With any luck, he'd convince her to keep all of them—and the mama cat.

"Let's put them in the laundry room. They'll be fine there for now," Laura said. "We've got pee pads in the top cupboard over the washer. Spread those out and bring them a bowl of water. I've still got unopened cans of cat food."

"Will the kittens eat that?"

Laura shook her head. "They're too young. The mama

cat will need to eat—especially since she's nursing three kittens. Let's get them settled now. We'll take them to the vet tomorrow or the next day."

Ian headed for the laundry room with his box of vocal felines.

"I can't thank you both enough." Laura's voice cracked as she turned to Kurt and Clara.

Clara set Noelle on the floor and put her arms around Laura, drawing her into a hug. "I'm so sorry my dog got lost and started this whole nightmare," she whispered into Laura's ear.

Laura clutched her tightly. "Don't you dare think you're responsible," she whispered back.

Clara nodded and pulled away. "We'll talk later. Right now, we all need a meal and sleep." She picked up Noelle and she and Kurt left the house.

"Are you hungry?" Clara asked Kurt.

"Starved."

"Let's go to my place. I've got a wonderful loaf of sour-dough for toast, and I'll scramble us some eggs," she said as they walked to the guest house. "I'll call Maisie and Joan first to make sure they know Sweets & Treats will remain closed today. I'll ask Joan to tell the other employees."

They reached her still-unlocked door and stepped inside.

Clara lowered Noelle gently to the floor.

The canine headed directly for the kitchen and they heard her lapping water from her bowl.

"I'll feed Noelle and make coffee while you do that," Kurt said.

Clara placed her call to Maisie.

"Did you weather the storm cozy and warm inside that guest house of yours?" Maisie asked.

Clara filled her in on the night's activities that were anything but cozy and warm.

Maisie's exclamations punctuated Clara's account.

"Oh no!"

"That's awful."

And, "so scary."

"We've had a happy ending all around," Clara said. "That's all that matters. How did you and Josef fare?"

Maisie recounted their late-night trip to open the diner and bakery building to assist stranded motorists. It was now Clara's turn to be amazed.

"We've both had the most incredible night," Maisie said. "It's a good thing we're not opening the bakery today. We need the day off."

Clara's yawn was audible on the other end of the line.

"You need to tuck yourself into bed," Maisie said firmly. "I'll call Joan and the others. Leave it to me."

Clara walked into her bedroom. She sank onto the edge of her bed and shrugged out of her coat, letting it drop to the floor.

"I'd appreciate that, Maisie," Clara said, ending the call. She pulled the cap from her head and tossed it aside, lying back on the bed. Just for a minute, she thought. Then she'd take off her boots and head to the kitchen to fix breakfast.

Clara was asleep before she finished her thought.

～

KURT SIPPED his coffee as he stood at the kitchen window and surveyed the blanket of snow twinkling in the sun. He rubbed his hand over the stubble on his chin, hoping the caffeine from the coffee would kick in soon. If it didn't, he didn't think he'd stay awake long enough to eat breakfast.

Clara had been gone quite a while. She and Maisie must have gotten into a long conversation. He retrieved another mug from the cupboard and filled it with coffee. Clara was as beat as he was. He'd take her a cup.

Kurt padded down the hallway in his stocking feet, Noelle at his heels. Clara wasn't in the living room. He listened for the sound of her voice, but heard nothing.

Noelle headed for the open bedroom door. Kurt followed her, knocked lightly on the door frame, then stuck his head inside. Clara lay with her back on the bed and her feet on the floor. Her mouth was agape, and she snored softly.

Kurt walked to the bed, setting the cup of steaming coffee on the nightstand. "Hello, princess," he said.

Clara didn't respond.

Kurt lifted her right foot and unzipped her boot, slipping it off and placing it on the floor. He then removed the boot from her left foot.

Clara still didn't stir.

Kurt scooped up both legs and gently lifted them onto the bed. He picked up a down-filled throw that lay folded across the foot of the bed and shook it open. Kurt allowed it to float gently down on top of her. He tucked the throw around her and was lifting her head to place it on a pillow when her eyes fluttered open.

"Kurt," she said, her eyes unfocused. She tried to rise, but slipped back down. "I need to make you breakfast," she mumbled, forcing herself to consciousness.

"I'll take a rain check," Kurt said. "You're too exhausted to cook and I'm too beat to eat."

Clara shut her eyes and nodded.

"I brought you a cup of coffee," Kurt said. "It's on the nightstand—if you want it."

Clara shook her head.

"I'd better take off before I'm too tired to drive," Kurt said.

"You're not going anywhere in your current state." Clara opened her eyes, and they locked gazes. Her right arm shot up, and she grasped a fistful of his sweater, pulling him onto the bed next to her. Clara tugged at the down throw, positioning it so it covered them both.

Kurt placed his palm on her cheek and leaned toward her.

Their lips met.

Clara pushed her mouth against his, responding to his growing sense of urgency with her own.

She finally pushed herself back. "We're sleeping, not..." Clara murmured.

"I know. When we make love, it won't be when we're both so exhausted we're about to sink into unconsciousness."

"I agree." She put her head back onto her pillow.

He pulled the throw under his chin and was asleep shortly after Clara.

Noelle hopped onto the bed and wedged herself between Kurt and Clara, digging at the throw and pushing against Kurt with her head. When she'd finally cleared her space, she sank into her usual spot on the bed next to her mistress.

They soon filled the room with three distinctly different snores.

CHAPTER 27

*L*aura woke with a start to the buzzing of her cell phone. She lunged for it on her nightstand but knocked it to the floor. Laura groaned and threw back the covers, heaving herself out of bed. She fell to her knees and peered under the bed. Her phone was nowhere to be seen. Laura pressed her nose to the floor and looked under the nightstand. The phone, cradled by a nest of dust bunnies, buzzed again.

Laura fished the phone from its resting spot and tapped the screen to accept the call from the hospital. She brought it to her ear, her nose itching and twitching from the dust it brought with it.

"Ms. Ramsey?" The voice on the end of the line sounded serious. "We've been trying to reach you."

"I'm… I've been…" Laura's jaw tightened. "Is my grandmother all right? She sounded fine when I talked to her this morning."

"I'm her nurse. That's why I'm calling."

Laura's mouth went dry.

"They've released her." The nurse waited a beat. "To go home. She hasn't been able to get hold of you, so I said I'd try."

Laura glanced at the screen. She gulped when she saw she'd missed eight calls.

"You need to come get your grandmother. She's waiting for you."

"Of course," Laura said, relief flooding her voice. "I'm sorry I missed her calls." Laura dragged her hair off her face as she remembered her car remained in the hospital parking lot. "Tell her I'll be there as soon as I can."

"She's eager to go home."

"I understand." Laura jumped to her feet. "I'll be there as soon as I can find a ride." She disconnected the call before the nurse could comment.

Laura shoved her feet into the jeans that lay discarded at the foot of the bed. She pulled on her sweater and stepped to the window facing the street. If Kurt was still here, she'd ask him to drive her to the hospital.

Her heart sank when she saw the empty spot at the curb where his SUV had been.

She stuffed her feet into her shoes and opened the rideshare app on her phone. Laura entered the information for her trip to the hospital and groaned when she saw that no drivers were working. She bit her lip and was scrolling for Clara's number when her phone buzzed with an incoming call.

"Maisie," Laura said. "How are you?"

"Fine, dear. I talked to Clara and heard all about Tabitha and the horrible night you had. I hope I didn't wake you?"

"No. I was up."

"I'm wondering if I can drop off your dinner for tonight?"

"That would be so nice, but I don't want you out on these roads."

"Josef will bring me," Maisie said. "We live close by, and they've got most of the streets cleared by now."

Laura walked back to the window and pulled the curtain aside. They had cleared a single lane in her street.

"What time would work for you? The diner is closed today, so we're free all afternoon."

Laura cleared her throat. She hated to ask, but she was out of options. "Could I ask a favor?"

"Of course! We'd be happy to help."

"The hospital called, and they've released Tabitha. I need to bring her home, but I left my car in the hospital parking lot last night when Kurt picked me up after Ian went missing. It's a long story. Anyway—I can't find a rideshare and—"

"Josef would be more than happy to take you to the hospital."

Laura blew out a breath. "Thank you. That's a huge relief."

"She's ready now?"

"Yes. I gather she's been ready and is eager to come home."

"No one likes to be in a hospital longer than they have to." Maisie paused before continuing. "I've got a few things to finish for your dinner."

"Don't rush. Tabitha can wait a while longer."

"Absolutely not. Would you mind if I brought the ingredients and finished the prep in your kitchen?"

"That'd be wonderful." Laura sighed in relief. "Thank you so much, Maisie."

"Then it's settled. It'll take me fifteen minutes to gather everything up. We'll be at your house in just under half an hour."

"See you soon. You're a lifesaver," Laura said. She ended the call and headed for her bathroom, peeling herself out of the clothes she'd just donned. She'd spend fifteen minutes showering, brushing her teeth, and combing her hair. That would leave her ten minutes to let Ian know where she was going—and check on the cats.

Laura grunted as she turned on the hot water in the shower. A new cat and three kittens was not what she needed right now. But if Ian wanted them, he could keep them. She was so grateful to have him home, she'd have given him the moon if he'd asked for it.

Kurt rolled onto his side and inhaled deeply. The smell of frying bacon and fresh coffee filled his nostrils. He knew what he would find, but patted the side of the bed next to him anyway. It was empty.

He sat up slowly, bringing his feet to the floor. Kurt worked out regularly, but the unaccustomed exertion of the day before had caught up with him. He was sore in places he didn't know existed.

Clara was humming as she slipped thick slices of sourdough bread into the toaster.

Kurt walked stiffly to the kitchen and stood in the doorway, admiring her easy mastery of the room.

Clara looked up at him and smiled. "Good morning, sleeping beauty."

"I think that's supposed to be my line."

"Coffee?" Clara picked up the pot and filled the mug he'd brought with him from the bedroom. "Feeling better?"

"I'm rested, but every muscle aches."

"Me too. All that shoveling at Mr. Barnes' house did me

in." She cracked eggs into a pan. "What do you plan to do today?"

"I own the entire block of buildings that includes Sweets & Treats. I'd like to go down there to check for storm-related damage."

Clara's head popped up. "Can I tag along? I want to collect the mail and bring it back here. I've allowed it to stack up for at least a week."

Kurt grunted disapprovingly.

"I know—I know. I need to stay on top of things. We're planning our grand opening, and I got behind. Since I'm not open today, I'll have time to deal with it."

The toast popped up and Kurt crossed the kitchen to butter it. "I'd love it if you came with me," Kurt said. "Let's eat and we'll go."

"Perfect," Clara said, scooping scrambled eggs onto a plate and handing it to him. "And if there's any storm damage to my shop, I love that I'll have my landlord with me to complain to."

KURT DROVE SLOWLY along the street in front of Sweets & Treats. "All these front doors are obstructed by drifts. The leases obligate me to take care of snow removal. I'll call the company I use to make sure it's done by the morning."

"Thank you," Clara said. "I plan to be open for business tomorrow."

"I don't see any damage in front," Kurt said. "Let's drive behind the buildings." He swung the SUV into the alley. His four-wheel-drive handled the snowy terrain without a problem. They proceeded slowly along the back side of the row of buildings and stopped behind Clara's patisserie. "I need to have the alley plowed and to clear out everyone's parking space," he muttered.

"You're a very responsible landlord," Clara said. She dug into her purse for the keys to her shop and they got out of the SUV. She pushed through the snow to her employee entrance.

Kurt remained at the side of his SUV. His right hand cupped his eyes as he examined the roof line. A spot along the roof of the tenant two doors down from Clara caught his attention.

"Do you mind if I investigate something?" He pointed to the roof.

"No. Of course not." She reached her back door and kicked away the small drift in the doorway. Clara inserted her key and opened the door. "I'll leave this unlocked. Take your time and come in when you're done. I've got plenty to keep me occupied."

Kurt nodded, and they each got busy.

Clara made a thorough sweep of her premises, looking for any signs of water damage on the ceiling tiles or evidence of broken pipes. All was in order.

She assessed the state of the perishables in her refrigerator and freezers. They stored shelf-stable ingredients like flour and sugar in the freezer—not to preserve it, but to assure a consistent starting temperature of all ingredients in products that required a rise, like croissants. Everything was fine.

She and Joan had taken home all the eggs and butter. Clara had a small amount of milk and cream that she would have to throw away because the power had been out. She raised her hands over her head and stretched from side to side. The economic loss was negligible.

She unpacked an order of bakery boxes and arranged them by size below the display cases. Clara removed old newspapers from the rack by the front door and fed a new roll of paper into the cash register.

She walked into her tiny office and gathered up the mail. Three envelopes that she'd overlooked when they had arrived now caught her attention. One of them bore the return address of her divorce attorney. The other two were from her ex-husband's criminal attorney.

She took the scissors from the pencil cup on her desk and opened the one from her attorney. A cover letter informed her that her divorce from Travis was final and that final copies of all documents were enclosed. Clara stuffed everything back into the envelope. She was familiar with the contents and didn't need to go through it all again. She'd file it with her important papers. Clara closed her eyes and sighed. She was thankful this unhappy chapter in her life was over.

Next, she opened the two letters from the criminal attorney defending Travis on charges of insurance fraud. Apparently, he and his dental hygienist—the woman he'd been having an affair with—had been falsifying claims for reimbursement. Clara knew nothing about all that and didn't care. It was his problem, not hers.

She read the first one-page letter, and then the other. They both contained the same request. The only difference was the date at the top of the letter. Clara hadn't responded, so they'd written to her again.

She re-read the letters, her eyes growing wide in astonishment. They wanted her to agree to be deposed in his case. The defense lawyer wanted her to testify as a character witness—*in favor of Travis.*

She shook her head in utter disbelief. Hell would freeze over first.

She tore the letters into tiny pieces and shoved them into the trash can by her desk, pushing them forcefully to the bottom.

"Clara," Kurt called from her back door.

"In here," she called. She stacked the remaining unopened mail, placed it in a plastic bag stamped with the Sweets & Treats logo, and met him as he walked through the workroom.

"Everything good out there?" she asked.

"There's a small amount of damage to one roof. I've already called my maintenance guy. How's everything here?"

Clara inhaled deeply. "Fine. Couldn't be better."

CHAPTER 29

"You're lifesavers," Laura said to Josef and Maisie as she opened her kitchen door to them.

The elderly couple stepped inside. Josef's arms were loaded with grocery sacks, and Maisie carried a Crock-Pot.

"Good heavens," Laura said. "You've brought enough to feed an army."

"You've had a terrible time and you'll be busy caring for your grandmother. I figured I'd bring enough to see you through the rest of the week."

Laura took the Crock-Pot from Maisie and set it on the counter near an electrical outlet, then swept her former Girl Scout troop leader into a hug. "You're the most amazing person. I always wanted to grow up to be just like you." She leaned back and looked into Maisie's eyes. "I still do."

Maisie flushed with pleasure. "You might want to reserve judgment until you taste what I've brought."

"You're the best cook in Pinewood." Laura chuckled.

"Everyone knows that." She turned her attention to Josef. "Is there anything else to bring in?"

"Nope. We got it all."

"I'll go tell Ian we're on our way to the hospital," Laura said. "Be right back."

Josef and Maisie busied themselves unpacking the groceries.

Laura returned with Ian at her heels.

"Ian will help you with anything you need," Laura said to Maisie.

The boy hung back in the doorway, cuddling the gray kitten with the zigzag on his forehead.

Laura pulled her jacket and purse from their hook by the door and followed Josef out the door.

Maisie looked at Ian and smiled. "I think I can take it from here. You can continue whatever you were doing." She gestured to the kitten.

Ian shrugged. "I think Harry," he held up the kitten, "wants to go back to Ron and Hermione."

"You're a Harry Potter fan, are you?"

"Yes, ma'am," Ian said. "I wouldn't mind helping you, Mrs. Johanson."

"Call me Maisie—everyone does." She rested her palms against the counter. "Do you know how to cook?"

"Not really. I can make cereal and pop tarts. And stuff in the microwave."

"Would you like to learn how to make a few simple things from scratch?"

Ian nodded. "Mom gets home late sometimes and she's so tired, but she still has to fix dinner. Gran used to cook, but she can't anymore. I'd like to help."

"That's kind of you," Maisie said. "And very mature."

"I asked Mom to teach me to cook, but she hasn't had time. YouTube has some great videos, but I'm not sure where to start."

"Go put Harry with his siblings, and wash your hands. You can make the green salad for tonight's dinner."

Ian returned Harry to the laundry room and washed his hands.

"We've got several kinds of lettuce, a cucumber, tomatoes, and bell peppers. They all need to be cleaned and chopped." Maisie placed her knife case on the counter and unrolled it, revealing her collection of knives. "These are very expensive knives," she said. "They're very sharp."

"Our knives are dull. Mom says she needs to sharpen or replace them. Should I use one of ours?"

"No. A dull knife is more dangerous than a sharp one. I'm going to teach you basic knife skills so you won't cut yourself."

"That's cool. I've seen chefs on those videos. They go really fast."

"It takes a lot of practice to become that proficient. You'll work much more slowly." Maisie pulled the salad ingredients to the sink and instructed Ian in the proper way to wash them.

"Is it time for the knife yet?"

Maisie selected the same knife she'd handed to Kurt recently and showed Ian how to hold it and use it.

Ian worked his way methodically through all the salad vegetables, checking his grip once with Maisie and confirming the thickness of the cucumber slices.

"You're a natural," Maisie said. "Anyone would think you've been doing this for years."

Ian ceased chopping and looked at her. "For real?"

Maisie nodded. "Absolutely. You've achieved a uniform chop on everything. That's hard to do—no one does that on their first time."

Ian raised his eyebrows quizzically.

"I'm serious," Maisie replied. "Don't tell him I told you this, but you're way better than Kurt."

Ian guffawed.

"He came over to my house on Valentine's Day and I taught him how to make the same salad you're making. I'm being truthful. He did fine, but you could be very good."

A flush rose from Ian's collar to his ears. He finished prepping the vegetables.

"Would you like to learn how to make salad dressing? It's easy, and so much better than bottled."

"Sure. This is fun." Ian wiped his hands on a towel. "I'll help you all afternoon."

Maisie caught and held his gaze. "If there were a cooking school in Pinewood, would you enroll?"

He considered her question, then nodded. "If Mom said yes, I'd do it."

Maisie inhaled deeply, her thoughts far away.

Ian cleared his throat.

Maisie jerked her head back. There was a new twinkle in her eyes. "Right. Salad dressing. I brought a bottle of good olive oil." She pointed to where Josef had placed it on the counter. "Grab it and the balsamic vinegar next to it, and we'll get started."

CHAPTER 30

Ian answered Josef's knock on the kitchen door.

"Something sure smells good!" Josef said as he stepped inside.

"Banana chocolate chip muffins. For breakfast tomorrow morning," Maisie replied.

"We made an egg…" Ian turned to Maisie.

"Strata," she said, completing his sentence.

Josef looked around the kitchen. The trash was full of empty packaging. Cooling racks containing oatmeal raisin cookies spanned the countertops. A Bundt cake stood on an elevated plate, waiting to be iced.

"You've sure been busy," he said, a note of incredulity in his voice.

"You were gone quite a while," Maisie said.

"I stayed at the hospital until Laura called me to confirm they'd be on their way shortly," he replied. "I hope that was all right?"

"Perfectly," Maisie said. "We've been having a ball here.

Ian and I work together in a kitchen as well as Clara and I do," Maisie said. "He says he's never done any of this before, but I'm not so sure." She winked at Ian. "He's catching on quick."

"So my great-grandmother is on her way home?" Ian asked.

Josef nodded. "I thought I'd stay here until Tabitha is settled in. Sometimes the hospital sends you home with prescriptions to be filled. We could run those to the pharmacy for her."

The timer on the oven buzzed. Someone knocked firmly on the kitchen door, and they all turned.

"It's open," Ian called as he removed a muffin tin from the oven.

Clara and Noelle entered the room, followed by Kurt. He inhaled deeply. "It smells like heaven in here." Kurt carried the butter that had remained in Clara's cold car since the day before.

Clara held the two loaves of artisan bread and the bag of coffee. "We thought we'd drop these off for you," Clara said. She cast her eyes around the cluttered kitchen. "Is there room?"

Maisie opened the refrigerator door. "I can make space for them." She shifted items from one shelf to another, then motioned to Kurt and stepped aside.

He slipped the eggs and butter into place.

Noelle settled herself in the corner of the kitchen, hoping to snatch crumbs from the floor.

A sudden blast of cold air from the opening of the front door drew everyone's attention.

"That'll be Gran," Ian said. "She insists on coming in the front door." He deposited the second tray of muffins on the counter and ran to the door, Noelle yipping at his heels.

"I'll see if they need any help getting her into the house," Kurt said, leaving Maisie and Clara in the kitchen.

Clara stashed the coffee and bread in an open spot on the counter. "This all looks fabulous, Maisie. They'll be set for a week. And you were up half the night. I don't know how you did this."

"I couldn't have if Ian hadn't helped. He's an excellent student." Maisie gathered her knife case and the favorite whisk she'd brought with her and stowed them in her satchel. "I think we should clean up our mess and get out of here." Maisie stacked the cooled cookies into a container.

"I'll ask Kurt to take out the trash." Clara wrung out a dish rag under hot water and wiped the counters. "They'll want peace and quiet, now that Tabitha's home."

"I don't want peace and quiet." Tabitha stood in the doorway, leaning heavily on her cane, flanked by Ian and Kurt. "But I do want a decent meal. Hospital food is horrible!"

Maisie removed a cookie from the container and took it to Tabitha. "Would you like to sit at the table in the dining room to eat this?"

"Make it two of those sweet treats and you've got a deal."

"I'll fix you a cup of tea," Laura called to her grandmother as she entered the kitchen. "This all looks incredible, Maisie. I have to admit, I'm starved, too."

Maisie took another cookie from the container and

handed it to Laura. "I know it's only four-thirty, but everything's ready. You could eat dinner now, if you want to."

Laura filled the kettle and set it on the stove. She lit the burner and spun to face Maisie and Clara. "Will you stay and have dinner with us?"

"You don't want a crowd—" Maisie began.

Laura cut her off. "Josef told me how you opened the bakery building behind the diner for stranded motorists—and cooked for them. You didn't get home until the wee hours. Kurt and Clara were up all night searching for Ian and Noelle. Everyone deserves a good meal." She gestured around the room. "You've made a mountain of food."

"Thanks to Ian's help," Maisie said. "He's a remarkable young man."

Laura flushed with pride. "I'm learning more every day about how wonderful he is."

"Won't all the commotion be too tiring for Tabitha?"

"She complained all the way home about how bored she was at the hospital. I filled her in with the broad strokes of what went on and she can't wait to hear every detail." Laura looked at Maisie and shrugged. "You know how she is."

"One of the keenest minds and most curious people I know," Maisie said. "We'll stay on one condition."

"What's that?"

"We eat, clean up, and get out of your hair."

"Deal," Laura said as the kettle whistled. She placed a strainer full of tea leaves and poured boiling water into the cup. "Tabitha will be thrilled."

"Let's get the food on the table," Maisie said. "We'll serve family style."

Ian walked through the kitchen, Harry cuddled under his chin.

"Where are you going with that kitten?" Laura asked.

"I was going to show Gran," he said. "She loves cats."

Laura sighed and put a hand on her hip as she considered her boy and the kitten that would undeniably become part of their household.

Harry purred, a deep rumble for such a tiny cat.

Noelle inched forward and paused at Ian's feet, extending her nose cautiously toward his furry bundle.

Ian knelt. Harry stopped purring. The two animals brought their noses—nostrils flaring—slowly together. Noelle's back legs quivered.

The three women in the kitchen stopped what they were doing and watched the introduction.

Harry began purring again. Noelle relaxed and sat at Ian's feet.

"I think your great-grandmother has had enough excitement for one day. You can show your new kitten to her tomorrow," Laura said.

Ian stood, a smile spreading from ear to ear. "We're keeping Harry?"

"Of course we are. Now, put him back and help us get dinner on the table."

Clara resumed removing serving dishes from cupboards.

Ian returned to the kitchen and, working under Maisie's direction, dressed the salad and brought it to the table.

Maisie carved the pot roast that had been cooking in

the Crock-Pot all afternoon and arranged it on a platter, nestling vegetables and potatoes around the meat.

Ian set the table, where Tabitha was already installed, while Clara sliced a loaf of artisan bread and put it in a basket with a bowl of creamy butter.

"Where are Kurt and Josef?" Clara asked when Ian returned to the kitchen to get salt and pepper for the table.

"They're in the dining room. Gran's cross-examining them on all that happened since she left for the hospital."

"Everything ready?" Laura asked, bringing Tabitha's tea cup for a refill of hot water.

"It is," Maisie said.

"Great," Laura said. "I think the guys need rescuing from Gran. It's like the inquisition in there." Her smile of affection belied her words. She picked up the bread basket and exited, taking it and Tabitha's tea to the dining room.

Clara and Maisie stood on opposite sides of the kitchen counter. Clara scrutinized her business partner closely. Maisie sighed in deep satisfaction.

"Something's changed with you, hasn't it?" Clara tilted her head to one side.

Maisie didn't try to suppress the smile that came from her heart.

Clara rocked back on her heels. "You've decided what your next act is going to be, haven't you?"

Maisie's smile stretched even wider.

"Well?"

Maisie leaned toward Clara and lowered her voice. "I haven't told Josef yet."

"He'll support you—you know that."

Maisie nodded.

The two women locked eyes.

"I'd tell Rachel," Maisie said, her eyes growing moist, "so I'll tell you."

Clara swallowed the lump in her throat. She loved Maisie like she'd loved her own mother. Maisie's inference that she loved Clara like a daughter touched Clara to her core.

"I'm going to open a cooking school—in the old bakery building. Not a culinary institute. This won't be for chefs. It'll be a place where everyday people can be taught the skills we used to learn from our mothers and grand-mothers."

"That's a genius idea," Clara said.

"There's such a need. And I'm a good teacher."

"You're an excellent teacher."

"We'll make meals for students to take home and we'll deliver to homebound people. Maybe I can even offer classes through Pinewood High School. Cooking is chem-istry, after all."

"Wow. This sounds wonderful."

"I've been thinking about nothing else the past few days."

"Do you have a name for this school?"

"*Good Food - Great Life.*" Maisie sucked in a breath. "What do you think?"

Clara's smile now matched Maisie's. "I love it."

The kitchen door opened, and Ian stepped between them. "I'll bring in the roast. Everyone's ready to eat." He picked up the platter and returned to the dining room.

Maisie went to Clara and kissed her cheek. "I'll tell Josef

in the morning. Can you come over tomorrow night to help me make plans?"

"You can count on me, Maisie." *Always*, Clara thought, as they walked into the dining room to join the people who had become her new family.

THE END

THANK YOU FOR READING!

If you enjoyed *Snowflakes, Cupcakes & Kittens*, I'd be grateful if you wrote a review.

Just a few lines on Amazon or Goodreads would be great. Reviews are the best gift an author can receive. They encourage us when they're good, help us improve our next book when they're not, and help other readers make informed choices when purchasing books. Goodreads reviews help readers find new books. Reviews on Amazon keep the Amazon algorithms humming and are the most helpful aide in selling books! Thank you.

To post a review on Amazon:

1. Go to the product detail page for *Snowflakes, Cupcakes & Kittens* on Amazon.com.

2. Click "Write a customer review" in the Customer Reviews section.

3. Write your review and click Submit.

THANK YOU FOR READING!

In gratitude,
  Barbara Hinske

ACKNOWLEDGMENTS

I'm blessed with the wisdom and support of many kind and generous people. I want to thank the most supportive and delightful group of champions an author could hope for:

My remarkable husband, Brian Willis, who never fails to steer me away from the rocks when ideas fail me;

My insightful and supportive assistant Lisa Coleman who keeps all the plates spinning;

My life coach Mat Boggs for your wisdom and guidance;

My kind and generous legal team, Kenneth Kleinberg, Esq., and Michael McCarthy—thank you for believing in my vision;

The professional "dream team" of my editors Linden Gross, Kelly Byrd, and proofreader Dana Lee;

Elizabeth Mackey for a beautiful cover.

ABOUT THE AUTHOR

USA Today Bestselling Author BARBARA HINSKE is an attorney and novelist. She's authored the Guiding Emily series, the mystery thriller collection "Who's There?", the Paws & Pastries series, two novellas in The Wishing Tree series, and the beloved *Rosemont Series*. Her novella *The Christmas Club* was made into a Hallmark Channel movie of the same name in 2019. A screen adaptation of *Guiding Emily* is scheduled to be released in 2023.

She is extremely grateful to her readers! She inherited the writing gene from her father who wrote mysteries when he retired and told her a story every night of her childhood. She and her husband share their own Rosemont with two adorable and spoiled dogs. The old house keeps her husband busy with repair projects and her happily decorating, entertaining, and gardening. She also spends a lot of time baking and—as a result—dieting.

ENJOY THIS EXCERPT FROM GUIDING EMILY

Prologue

Emily. The woman who would become everything to me. The person I would eat every meal with and lie down next to every night—for the rest of my days.

She was just ahead; behind that door at the far end of the long hall. I glanced over my shoulder. Mark kept pace, slightly behind me. I could feel his excitement. It matched my own.

Everyone said Emily and I would be perfect for each other. I'd overheard them talking when they thought I was asleep. I spend a lot of time with my eyes closed, but I don't sleep much. They didn't know that.

"A magical match," they'd all agreed.

I lifted my eyes to Mark, and he nodded his encouragement. I gave a brief shake of my head. Only four more doorways between Emily and me.

I picked up my pace. A cylindrical orange object on the carpet in the third doorway from the end caught my eye. *Is that a Cheeto? A Crunchy Cheeto? I love Crunchy Cheetos.*

I tore my eyes away.

This was no time to get distracted.

We sped across the remaining distance to the doorway at the end of the hall. The door that separated me from my destiny.

I froze and waited while Mark knocked.

I heard Emily's voice—the sound I would come to love above all others—say, "Come in."

What was that in her voice? Eagerness—anxiety—maybe even a touch of fear? I'd take care of all of that right away.

The door swung open and Mark stepped back. He pointed to Emily.

I'd seen her before. Emily Main was a beautiful young woman in her late twenties. Auburn hair cascaded around her shoulders and shone like a new penny. With my jet-black coloring, we'd make a striking couple.

"Go on," Mark said.

I abandoned all my training—all sense of decorum—and raced to her.

Emily reached for me and flung her arms around my neck.

I placed my nose against her throat, and she tumbled out of her chair onto her knees.

I swept my tongue over her cheek, tasting the saltiness of her tears.

"Oh … Garth." My name on her lips came out in a hoarse whisper.

I wagged my tail so hard that we both lay back on the floor.

"Good boy, Garth!"

She rubbed the ridge of my skull behind my ears in a way that would become one of my favorite things in the whole wide world.

Next to food.

Especially Crunchy Cheetos.

Mark and the other trainers were right—we were made for each other. I was the perfect guide dog for Emily Main.

Chapter 1

"Weren't you supposed to leave for the airport half an hour ago?" Michael Ward asked his boss, whose fingers were typing furiously on her keyboard. "You're still planning to get married, aren't you?"

Emily Main's head bobbed behind the computer, her eyes fixed to the screen.

"I can't believe you put off a departure to Fiji to help us launch this new program. Your wedding's in two days."

"We've been working on this for almost a year. I wasn't about to leave when we're this close. I just need to finish this last email." She hunched forward and peered at the computer screen.

"There," she said, pushing her office chair back as the email *whooshed* from her inbox. "Done."

She looked up at Michael, blinking. It was probably the first time she had looked at anything besides a computer screen in hours. "I brought my suitcase so I could go to the airport straight from the office. I don't have to stop at home."

Michael raised his eyebrows at her. "That's all you've got? A carry-on and a satchel for a week—a week that includes your wedding? My wife packs more than that for a three-day weekend."

"My wedding dress is a classic sheath and the rest is bathing suits and shorts."

"I would have thought Connor Harrington the third would have wanted an elaborate wedding—one fit for the society pages."

"Our wedding is going to be very elegant—think JFK Junior and Carolyn," Emily said, flinging her purse over her shoulder and reaching for the retractable handle of her suitcase.

Michael stepped in front of her. "I've got this," he said. "I'll walk you to the street. I'd like to congratulate Connor on snagging our office hero."

Emily hesitated.

"He is picking you up, isn't he? You're flying there together?"

"He went out over the weekend. He wanted to do some diving with his best man … sort of a bachelor party reprise. I was traveling with my mom and maid of honor, but they flew out yesterday as planned. The company paid to change my ticket, but it would have cost almost five hundred dollars for Mom and Gina to change theirs. It wasn't worth it."

"But you don't like to fly." He peered into Emily's face. "Did you talk to Connor about that before you decided to stay an extra day? You have told him about your fear of flying, haven't you?"

Emily shrugged. "I've mentioned it, sure, but I haven't made a big deal out of it."

"So what did he say?"

"He suggested that I get a prescription for Xanax and sleep the whole way out there."

"Really? That's what he said?"

"He's a Brit, for heaven's sake. 'Stiff upper lip' and all that. He's not the sort of guy to coddle anyone—and I'm not a needy type of gal. You know that."

Michael cocked his head to one side. "Do you have to change planes?"

Emily nodded.

"You don't want to be knocked out for that."

"I'll be fine." Emily threw her shoulders back. "You don't need to worry about me."

"I know—I'm sorry. It's just that I wouldn't let my wife make the trip alone if she felt like you do about flying."

"I fly alone all the time, and nothing's ever happened to me. There's no reason this time should be any different."

Michael lifted his hands, palms facing her, and shrugged. "Okay, but I think he could have at least offered to pay to change your mom's flight or something."

"I'll be perfectly fine." Emily walked past him into the hallway. "I promised Dhruv that I'd say goodbye before I leave."

"He's going to miss you. You're the one person here that really connects with him."

Michael watched her shoulders sag slightly.

"Hey," he said, rolling the carry-on to a halt beside her in the hall. "I'm sorry. I didn't mean to worry you. The whole team is going to step into your shoes while you're gone. We've talked about it."

"Of course you will. I shouldn't worry about him. I've got the best team in San Francisco. Scratch that. On the entire West Coast." Emily gave him a teary smile and punched him playfully on the shoulder. "I know you'll take care of everything while I'm away, Michael—including helping Dhruv stay connected with the team."

"Good!" Michael continued down the hallway. "I don't want you to give this place a second thought while you're gone. If anyone deserves a vacation—and a gorgeous beach wedding—it's you, Em. But don't get too comfortable." Michael turned and smiled at her. "We do need you to come back. We'd be lost without you here."

Emily laughed and pushed him toward the elevator. "Why don't you go push that button, you wonderful suck-up. It'll take ages to get an elevator this time of the morning. I'll stick my head into Dhruv's cubicle and be right back."

***

Emily found Dhruv, as usual, leaning into the bank of computer monitors, intently focused on the complex strings of code in front of him. She cleared her throat. When Dhruv didn't move, she tapped him lightly on the shoulder.

Dhruv sat back quickly and spun around. A smile spread across his face when he saw her.

"I wanted to say goodbye before I go."

Dhruv nodded. "Goodbye."

"I'll see you a week from Monday."

"I know. You're getting married in two days, then you have your honeymoon for a week, then you come back to work," he recited.

"That's right. You remembered."

"I remember things."

"Yes, you do. That's one reason you're so very good at programming," she said.

"I know."

"Okay … well … have a good week. You can go to Michael if you have … if you need anything."

"I know."

Emily regarded the shy, socially awkward middle-aged man who was, by far, the most proficient member of her extremely talented team of programmers. "Bye."

Dhruv nodded.

Emily stepped away.

Dhruv leapt out of his chair and called after her. "Have a happy wedding."

Emily swung around and gave him a thumbs-up then turned back toward the elevators where Michael was waiting.

From *Guiding Emily*

CONNECT WITH BARBARA HINSKE ONLINE

Sign up for her newsletter at **BarbaraHinske.com**
Goodreads.com/BarbaraHinske
Facebook.com/BHinske
Instagram/barbarahinskeauthor
TikTok.com/BarbaraHinske
Pinterest.com/BarbaraHinske
Twitter.com/BarbaraHinske
Search for **Barbara Hinske on YouTube**
bhinske@gmail.com

Available at Amazon in Print, Audio, and for Kindle

The Rosemont Series

Coming to Rosemont

Weaving the Strands

Uncovering Secrets

Drawing Close

Bringing Them Home

Shelving Doubts

Restoring What Was Lost

No Matter How Far

When Dreams There Be

Novellas

The Night Train

The Christmas Club (adapted

for The Hallmark Channel, 2019)

Paws & Pastries

Sweets & Treats

Snowflakes, Cupcakes & Kittens

Workout Wishes & Valentine Kisses

Wishes of Home

Novels in the Guiding Emily Series

Guiding Emily

The Unexpected Path

Over Every Hurdle

Down the Aisle

Novels in the "Who's There?!" Collection

Deadly Parcel

Final Circuit

www.ingramcontent.com/pod-product-compliance
Lightning Source LLC
Chambersburg PA
CBHW020340010826
48970CB00012B/2317